Rajeev Bhargava is a creative author whose books and stories include dark-fantasy and horror, science-fiction and fantasy, an *Assorted Poems: Haikus Collection* on themes including love and romance, comedy, wit, and humour as well as the welfare of animals, plants and love, admiration and concern for our green environment. And, just recently, he published a children's storybook for Christmas, Easter and Halloween, all previously under the pen name Silver Phoenix. Rajeev absolutely loves all forms of art and creativity, attaining a BA (HONS) in Literature Degree and an English Literature Teaching Certificate, but enjoys writing the most.

I would like to dedicate my horror book to several famous and respected people:

First, with respect to the very talented, late, and great filmmaker, American Willard Tobe Hooper - director, producer, and screenwriter; best known for his work in horror movies. I loved his movie 'The Funhouse' and the multi-talented and inspirational Damien Leone, the famous film director, film producer, and screenwriter for his horror trilogy featuring Art the Clown. Thank you so much for the classic horror 'Terrifier' trilogy. I applaud and love all your movies and the actors in them. I believe you are simply the best modern horror filmmaker and have won my admiration and respect for life. May you grow from strength to strength. Takashi Shimizu, the Japanese director for his classic movie, 'The Grudge,' which I love. Takashi Shimizu the Japanese director for his classic movie, 'The Grudge' Japanese actors Satsuko Hara and Toshiro Mifune, Japanese director Yoshimitsu Banno. I love 'Godzilla vs Hedorah' (or Godzilla vs the Smog Monster). John Carpenter, the filmmaker, actor, and composer. I love 'The Fog' and 'Christine.' And last, but by no means least, Stephen King, whom I regard as simply the greatest modern-day horror writer. I love 'Carrie.'

Silver Phoenix

TERRIFYING AND BLOOD

Curdling Stories for...Sshh!!...
It's Halloween...

Austin Macauley Publishers™
LONDON • CAMBRIDGE • NEW YORK • SHARJAH

Copyright © Silver Phoenix 2024

The right of Silver Phoenix to be identified as author of this work has been asserted by the author in accordance with sections 77 and 78 of the Copyright, Designs and Patents Act 1988.

All rights reserved. No part of this publication may be reproduced, stored in a retrieval system, or transmitted in any form or by any means, electronic, mechanical, photocopying, recording, or otherwise, without the prior permission of the publishers.

Any person who commits any unauthorised act in relation to this publication may be liable to criminal prosecution and civil claims for damages.

This is a work of fiction. Names, characters, businesses, places, events, locales, and incidents are either the products of the author's imagination or used in a fictitious manner. Any resemblance to actual persons, living or dead, or actual events is purely coincidental.

A CIP catalogue record for this title is available from the British Library.

ISBN 9781035819874 (Paperback)
ISBN 9781035819881 (Hardback)
ISBN 9781035819904 (ePub e-book)
ISBN 9781035819898 (Audiobook)

www.austinmacauley.com

First Published 2024
Austin Macauley Publishers Ltd®
1 Canada Square
Canary Wharf
London
E14 5AA

I would like to wholeheartedly thank each and every respected member of the Austin Macauley Publishers team and my production coordinator for their assistance in my book reaching publication. A very special thank you to my Acquisitions Editorial Assistant for providing me with that extra inspirational spark with her kind comments on the review of my book and its potential to be a great horror classic. Thank you all very much indeed.

Table of Contents

Beelzebub's Mausoleum of Spectres	13
The Spirit of All Hallow Eve	19
Crepuscular Fiend	20
Dicing with Libitina, Goddess of Funerals and Burials	27
'Shadow Sheila' and Her 'Abettor'	28
Zuguh: Abomination from Hell!	37
The Deceased Cubicle of Succubus	47
Where the Qori Ismaris Abides	54
"Blood Blood"	60
And Now for My Next Trick	73
'Cutting Down'	76
Zom-Bait	86
Clown Cemetery	92
Beware of the Wendigos!	99
Hafhogr Egod AD	100

Brass Mineral Lighthouse Hospice for the Terminally 'Undead'	107
Libitina, Goddess of Funerals and Burials	115
That Old Derelict High School	116
Rest in 'Pieces'	130
Cinema Screaming	131
Demon-Priest	142
Tiara, Zombie-Girl	143
Frenzic Bite	152
Charaal	153
The Gates of Hell	158
The Witching Seed	159
Beware, the Undead	164
Nachzehrer, Lonesome and on the Prowl	165
Strigoi: Grand-Daddy of All Vampires	166
Skyrim, Headless Horseman	167
Right Time Right Place	168
Death Call: A Samurai Ghost's Recollection of His Death	172
(Japanese Haiku-Poem)	172
Yokai	173
Hallowed Cauldron	181
The Bleached Eyes of a Torn Soul	191

Witches' Blood	**193**
Wail of the Scarecrow	**195**
Duppy	**196**

Beelzebub's Mausoleum of Spectres

"Roll up; roll up, ladies and gentlemen! Witness, if you *dare,* Beelzebub's mausoleum of spectres right here through these gates of hell. Step right on inside."

An athletic, caped figure, dressed in a red satanic outfit and mask, holding a long red fork looked around at onlookers as they just walked by, passing glances, giving shrugs and waives of disbelief, then shuffling along to enjoy the late-night carnival. It was nearing midnight, and the figure sat down on a stool, head bowed.

"Say, that's one creepy outfit you have on. And if what you say is *real*, then what guarantee do I have that *I'll* make it back out alive and in one piece?" The showman raised his head and stood up instantly. A burly man of average height stood before him, dressed smartly in a three-piece navy and grey suit. He wore a matching black tie.

"Oh, I can assure you; you will *definitely* come out in one piece." His peering green eyes appeared to glow straight through his red skin-mask as he gave an evil grin. "This way, please, Mister…"

"Edwin Woodburgh," he replied, his left eye starting to twitch, as they proceeded through red gates.

A long creepy barren trail surrounded by bare trees lay ahead and a red smoky mist rose and slowly seeped from the ground and blocked his vision.

"It's...intimidating to say the least. So, where is this mausoleum?"

"We're on its outskirts. It's straight ahead." The showman pointed a creepy finger that ended with a black talon. "Just follow me very closely."

As they continued onwards, Edwin felt the hair follicles on his arms rise as he heard a loud eerie howl.

"What was that? It...it sounded like a wolf."

"Oh, really, Mr Woodburgh, why do you act so surprised when you know full well that we are inside the mausoleum! It's merely a werewolf on its night-hunt. Here, you will witness, and eventually encounter, the most heinous and horrific monsters that ever roamed our planet."

"Yes, I...I can see why you have problems attracting visitors now." Edwin felt his forehead perspire and loosened his tie, then undid the top button of his shirt. He began to feel nauseous and suddenly lost his balance and fell to the ground. Darkness followed...

*****

When Edwin regained consciousness, he felt a terrible pounding sensation. It was as if someone was hammering inside his skull. He looked up, wide-eyed, but could not move freely. It was pitch black.

"W...where am I? Get me out of here! Help!" He felt himself gasping for air, realising he was trapped inside a container of some sort. After a while, he heard footsteps approaching. In desperation, he began to yell out and scratched the container's surface but his nails broke in the process.

The footsteps stopped and he heard someone crouching next to him and attempting to open the lid. He could hear the sound of his heart beating faster and faster in anxiety...

Suddenly, the lid flung aside and he took deep gasps of air, staring wide-eyed in shock and disbelief at the same satanic figure before him. Edwin stood up and got out.

"Y...you're crazy. You tried to kill me. Just wait until I get out of this place. You won't be working in any night carnival again; I can assure you of that!"

"Come come, Mr Woodburgh, surely you're not going to let my little stunt scare you away! Why, I haven't yet even introduced you to the residents of my mausoleum."

"That's good, because quite frankly, I don't care anymore. Now, if you would be kind enough to escort me back to the carnival, I wish to lodge a complaint."

Suddenly, there was a loud distant thud, followed by scraping sounds. Edwin turned to him in fear.

"W...what's that sound?" There was no response from the satanic figure, so he turned to leave, but his path was blocked by his fork. It tipped his right arm and seared it. His coat caught fire and he removed it instantly and tossed it on the ground.

"I forbid you to go anywhere until you have met my children." Just then, Edwin became curious.

"Wait a minute. Who are you? I demand you remove that mask and show me your face. I think you've gone too far."

"All in good time, Mr Woodburgh. But I want to remind you that you did come here at your own peril."

"For heaven's sake, this is supposed to be part of your carnival act, so why are you acting so strange?"

And then, from out of the red mist, a giant eight-foot medieval stone man appeared.

"Ah, they're starting to awaken now. Meet one of my…err…residents shall we say?"

"It's some kind of living statue."

"In your history books, it is better known as a Golem," he replied, smiling wickedly. The Golem continued walking closer and closer towards Edwin, who began retreating backwards.

"Make it stop. Please," he said as the Golem reached out its arms towards him, slowing down. The figure snapped his fingers and it turned directions and walked off and vanished in the mist.

"Alright, I've had enough of this sick nonsense. I'm warning you, for the first and last time, to take off your mask…now!"

"How dare you threaten the lord of darkness!" he replied, infuriated. Just then, Edwin leapt forwards at the satanic figure and placed both his hands tightly around his throat.

"Y…you're choking…me, you fool!" Edwin released his grip, then instantly went for the mask. Both his eyes were flickering. He was hysterical. When it did not come off, he began to rip and claw at it.

Just then, he let go and retreated back in disbelief, suspicion and finally, horror.

"Oh, God. That's…your real face! It means…you must be…Satan himself!"

The satanic figure, his face oozing with bloody scratches, reached for his fork and stood up wearily, managing a grin. A grin that soon turned to a loud burst of manic laughter.

"Hah hah hah hah hah hah hah! Hah hah hah hah hah hah hah!" Edwin stood transfixed, finding himself unable to move anything but his head.

"Perfect!" he quipped, then took a full circle around Edwin. "Now the time has come to summon all my spectres." Momentarily, he turned his back on Edwin, and raised both his arms up, his cape blowing to and fro and then murmured a few words in what sounded like an ancient dialect.

In one last bid to free himself, Edwin protested.

"D...don't forget your promise. You said I would make it back out alive and in one piece."

"Oh, yes, so I did. And I'm upholding that promise, Mr Woodburgh; once my children of the dark have had their way with you, *you will make it out in one piece.*"

Suddenly, from out of the red mist, figures of all shapes and sizes began to appear, and made their way towards Edwin. Demons, goblins, mummies, witches, ghouls, vampires and werewolves and zombies to name a few that had picked up the scent of their new bait. Edwin's eyes grew wide in pure terror as he tried to move, but he could not budge an inch. But then, to his relief and surprise, they stopped and hesitated, appearing petrified and then began to retreat backwards, cautiously, disappearing from where they came. The satanic figure laughed and then turned to Edwin and whispered in his left ear.

"Well, it was an interesting observation to say the least. Look, you even frightened them all away."

"W...what do you mean?" Edwin said.

"Oh, you're not worthy to stay here in my mausoleum because you happen to be the most frightening and deadly of all the dark species-a MAN! No one can ever commit such atrocities as your kind. Your entire history is filled with violence and blood; a lot more than the marks you put on my face. That's why I'm going to give you something you have earned." He aimed his fork straight at Edwin and flung it into his neck. Darkness followed...

*****

"Roll up; roll up, ladies and gentlemen! Witness, if you *dare,* Beelzebub's mausoleum of spectres right here through these gates of hell. Step right on inside."

The athletic, caped figure, dressed in a red satanic outfit and mask, stood firmly, holding a long red fork, looking at onlookers as they just walked by, but this time, they stopped, and began crowding around him in excitement for on the tip of the fork was the impaled head of Edwin Woodburgh.

There were no eyes, only sockets. It even called out, in a pained voice, from its bloodied mouth, "Help me...help me."

"Wow!" called out a lady in the night crowd, "it looks so creepy and real!"

The End.

The Spirit of All Hallow Eve

Trick or treat, disguised as the undead, partying the night away at Halloween functions, sharing scary and spooky stories that make your toes curl-Candy Pumpkins, Bonfire Toffee and Monkey Nuts: ghosts and spirits looming about freely in the dead of night…

Crepuscular Fiend

The huge red and black-bricked mansion stood elegantly in all its grandeur in the remote countryside, amidst the cold bare trees, appearing like a relic from a long time ago. However, it had an eerie past, so was considered haunted. Rumours had spread that its 'occupant' was something so horrid that nobody dared set foot inside. In fact, if anyone even glanced at it would suffer a 'bad fate' in their lifetime.

"Very impressive!" quipped the attractive young lady tourist, in her mid-twenties, as she stopped in her tracks, across the winding pathway, to catch sight of it.

"*Don't look at it, Jelena!*" Called out her partner, a lanky spectacled man in his late thirties. She giggled and placed her hands into his.

"Oh, don't be so jumpy, Andy. I'm going to go inside; come on!"

In a last desperate bid, he clasped her hands and pleaded with her.

"*Please*. If you care for my feelings, then let's just move on. Besides, I'm sure there are bound to be other places where we can lodge in."

"You must be joking! My feet have got blisters walking continually for hours. Besides, this was all your idea, to find a nice spot where you can pick up ideas for your new book. Now, are you coming or not?"

"Well, don't say I didn't warn you. We both know about the rumours that revolve around that creepy place."

"Creepy! Just look at it. It's so beautiful and majestic. I always dreamed of living in a place like this."

This time, Jelena did not wait for his response and made her way forwards.

Andy shrugged, then began following her, nervously.

They continued up the narrow black and red granite trail leading to the main door.

"There, that wasn't so difficult now, was it, Andy, hmm?" She prodded him in his abdomen with her left hand and giggled.

"Ouch. Hah, hah, very amusing."

The door was well polished with a thick green and black paint.

"One thing is for certain, Andy, the occupant is very particular about maintaining the beauty of this place. Now, let's go in."

"No, wait!" Andy said, "We can't just walk in!"

"Honestly, did you *really* think I was going to do that! Duh!" She searched around for the doorbell or a door handle. There wasn't any.

"How odd!" Jelena said. Suddenly, the heavy door opened partially. There was just enough space for them to go in. Once inside, the door slammed shut and there was the sound of a heavy bolt.

"Oh, now you've really done it. We're locked in! See, I did warn you!" Andy cried. He began to bang the door. "Help! Help!"

Jelena slapped him hard on his left cheek.

"Stop it at once! You're such a big baby. Honestly! I know it was my idea, so I take full responsibility to get us both out of here. Just trust me, alright?"

He nodded.

"Good. Now, take a deep breath and follow me."

It was very sombre, murky and unlit. Everything appeared blurred and misty. So much so that neither of them could make out anything clearly.

Suddenly, something brushed against Andy and he jumped.

"Aaahhh!"

"What is it now, Andy!" Jelena yelled with a frown. "Just stop it or I'll go crazy!"

"Not you, Jelena, I'll go crazy! I'm not going a step further. Let's get out of this place."

Just then, a very melodious sound filled the air. It seemed to be coming from above. Jelena held Andy's right hand and began proceeding up the spiral stone stairs.

"Err, aren't we supposed to be going towards the main door, Jelena?"

Jelena ignored Andy's protests and continued up the long flight of stairs until a long shadow fell across the top step. Someone was approaching.

"There's still time. Quickly, let's hide!" Andy said nervously. He tugged himself free from Jelena and ran quickly back downstairs and vanished out of sight, in the dusk.

"Jelena Crepson! Long time no see!"

"Aunt Wertila! What a pleasant surprise!"

A very tall, slim and attractive lady with long scarlet hair stood at the top of the stairs and ushered Jelena upstairs.

Jelena smiled and followed her aunt along the corridor. Along the way, the darkness turned to an illuminating yellow light. In a few seconds, the colour changed to orange, then blue, yellow and green.

"Oh, that's beautiful!" Jelena remarked.

Aunt Wertila smiled. "The colours will keep changing. They're fluorescent."

"Excuse me, Aunty, I'll be right back." Jelena turned back to the stairs and called out at the top of her voice.

"Andy! Come on up and meet Aunt Wertila. Andy!"

There was no reply.

"Wait, let me summon him," said Aunt Wertila.

She snapped her left hand and in an instant, Andy appeared before them from out of the air. He looked around, confused.

"How did you do *that*, Aunty?" Jelena asked.

"I've had this gift since birth. I never told a soul." She tapped her nose and smiled.

"Come on, I'll show you both to your rooms."

"S…see, Jelena. I told you. Woof woof woof!" Andy held his throat and turned to her, wide-eyed. "Wuff…wuff!"

"Leave us in peace, you bad brat!" Stormed Aunt Wertila.

She grabbed Andy's left ear and took him to one of the side rooms and pushed him inside, then bolted the door. She then smiled, straightened her crimson gown and walked back to Jelena, who watched, wide-eyed.

"Was that really necessary, Aunt Wertila?"

"Oh, the effect will wear off in a couple of hours. Now, follow me. I'm dying to show you something."

They soon arrived at a large green door with a purple skull on it. Aunt Wertila opened the door and as she stepped into the room, turned invisible.

"Come and find me!" She called out to Jelena.

Jelena stepped inside, then found she could not move. She gazed down at her feet and they were literally glued to the carpet. She looked around and called out:

"That's not funny, Aunty. Please release me."

There was no reply. Just pin-drop silence. Jelena began to sob and repent her adamant nature to go inside.

"I'm…sorry, Andy. I should have listened to you."

Just then, she heard a loud thud. It came from the corridor.

"Andy? Andy, I'm in here!"

Just then, a large shadow fell across the floor, followed by heavy breathing. In a desperate bid to free herself, Jelena closed her eyes tightly, then crouched to the floor and heaved upwards with all her force.

"Aaahhhh!" Her body jetted into the air and fell sideways on the hard concrete floor. Darkness followed…

When her eyes opened, Jelena found Andy kneeling over her with a look of concern.

"A…Andy. You're alright. What happened?"

"No, don't get up, Jelena. Stay as you are."

"Why?" She looked around to observe her surroundings.

"We're in the basement; that's where your beloved aunt locked me in. I used my canine strength to knock the blasted door down." As he spoke, saliva dribbled down his mouth onto the floor.

"Ewww!" Jelena said, as some landed on her legs. She also noted he had paws.

"Andy! Where are your feet?"

"Oh, wake up, Jelena, for goodness' sake...wuff wuff!" He coughed. A moment's silence, then she began to giggle and paused.

"Andy, you've not only changed into a hybrid, but you've also become more aggressive."

"I know." Andy lowered his head, feeling ashamed. "I can't help it. Your Aunt Wertila put some kind of a spell on me. Wuff wuff."

Jelena thought hard.

"If we make an escape, you'll remain this way for good. There's only one way out. We will have to give ourselves in to Aunt Wertila and plead with her."

"I somehow don't think that's a very good idea, Jelena."

Suddenly, the door of the basement flung open.

"There you are!" yelled Aunt Wertila. "Come on out...both of you. Now!"

Both Andy and Jelena made their way out of the basement and followed her into a chamber room. But as her dress brushed against the door, it got caught around its spiked edges and tore off to reveal something that left them aghast...

Andy instinctively covered Jelena's eyes.

The lower half of Aunt Wertila's body was that of a snake and her skin was made up of scales and speckles.

"What is it, Andy?" Jelena cried out, wide-eyed.

"I don't know, Jelena, but it's definitely not human!"

"*Correct!* Called out a pained voice from behind them. It's an Echidna!"

An icy slimy hand fell across Jelena's right shoulder.

"Aaaaaahhhhhhh!"

"Ruff!! Ruff!" Called out Andy and turned to give the Echidna a vicious bite.

"No, please don't. Like your, I too have been locked inside here for the past twenty years. This was my home until *that* monstrosity found a way in and has been feeding off my flesh as the prime source of nourishment…and now…she's going to get you too! Quickly, let's get out of here, Jelena. Or else that monstrosity is going to chew us up alive!"

Andy held her hand tightly and made a run for the main door. The Echidna hissed and slid forwards, but was held back by her tail.

"Let go of me, you fool."

"No. I can't let you harm them. This is my home and you kept me as a pet zombie, but…there's still some human consciousness left in me. That is it." Her eyes turned a deep green in anger and she opened her mouth to reveal razor sharp teeth.

"Goodbye!" Then she leant forwards and bit into his chest, pulling out his heart. She chomped at it and swallowed. Blood oozed and dribbled down her lips onto the floor.

In the meantime, Jelena had managed to find a large candle stand on the mantle and bashed open the bolted door. They were free…

But little did they realise a small group of Echidnas waiting to feast on them amidst the tall dark trees that surrounded the outskirts of the manor…

The End.

Dicing with Libitina, Goddess of Funerals and Burials

In the dead of night, in the corner of a desolate space, in pin-drop silence, a cloaked figure, with a scythe, sat crouched, clenching a dice in her hands but the 'numerals' etched on it were symbols representing her victim's fate.

The Grim Reaper reached out her bony left hand, then tossed it to the ground and looked across and gazed at her victim, sneering at his helplessness.

The victim, a young man in his twenties, sat petrified and frozen, awaiting his fate; the sweat pouring profusely down his forehead.

The dice span magically, in slow-motion on the wet ground, turning blood-red, ultimately revealing his fate; to be punished in a blaze of flames, but that would only be the finale: after each of his limbs were twisted off very slowly, ensuring he lived and endured all essence of the pain she inflicted, because for him, Death was the merciful release of his punishment for Dicing with LIBITINA, Goddess of Funerals and Burials...

'Shadow Sheila' and Her 'Abettor'

"Let me out of here! Let me out! I'm not crazy. Can anyone hear me?" She cried out, scratching at the thick padded walls of her isolated cell.

The agitated voice belonged to a frail young lady, aged twenty-two. Her true name remained anonymous since the first day when she was captured by the staff, last winter, running in the untamed woodlands that surrounded the centuries old mental institution aptly named **Mystic Woods Mental Institution**. Apparently, they believed she was a lycanthrope as they caught her, using a net, licking a blood-soaked human skull; where she found it, only she knew, and she wouldn't tell.

Over the years of her imprisoned confinement, she had been kept away in a pitch-black, sound-proof cell, isolated from other patients, due to her estranged habit of claiming to communicate with ghostly apparitions that moved around on the walls. This had a negative and disturbing impact on the entire staff, including the remaining inmates who would previously cover their faces and hold their ears pacing up and down, some crouching on the floor, as she would start to scream and roar like a wolf. This was brought to the immediate notice of the head of the institute, elderly dignified and formal man of ninety-seven, named Dr Hans Ghoulder who ordered her to be confined indefinitely in the 'deepest and darkest corner' effective as of now and stressed to all staff to enter her cell in pairs at all times.

Still frantic, she stormed to one corner of her imprisonment and fell on the cold floor, barefoot, then began sobbing. In frustration, she began to yell and tear at her already torn and tattered rag-dress. But now, as she was seemingly forgotten and out of sight, nobody noticed or cared. She stood up again, abruptly then pounced to the door.

Sheila 'X' then stretched out her hands, like a she-wolf and purred menacingly, after which she frantically began to scratch and claw at the padding of the entrance door. So much so, that her nails filled with blood and left impressions on the material on her fists and she began to hem with all her might, but it was no use. The padding was very thick which made it soundproof. She then flexed and curved her hands.

"Hooowwl! Hooowwl! This is one angry she-wolf." She growled in a violent and vehement frenzy and then began to scratch the cloth with such force that her already bitten nails filled with streaks of blood which oozed out from her nerves. In frustration, she spat at the door then returned back to the back-right corner of her cell and cupped her face, crying.

"You'll be sorry for what you did to me, you heartless monsters! Sob…Sob. I know you can all hear me; you're just pretending you can't…" Her voice was pained and faded away in pin-drop silence.

Just then, a bright and brilliant red glow appeared and filled the entirety of the right-side wall.

"What's happening? G…get away from me!"

And then before her very eyes, it began to form into a slender and sleek shape and shadow of a female figure, who sat cross-legged.

Her fear soon turned to fascination and curiosity got the better of her as she walked right up to it and stared hard at it. But when she reached out to touch it, the shadow instantly moved to a further side of the wall, as if frightened itself, then upwards at the ceiling.

"Hey! I thought *I* was the frightened one."

She sat on the floor, cross-legged and placed her hands on her cheeks, indicating boredom.

"I don't know why you run away from me. I mean, I can't harm you. I just want someone to talk to…a friend. You see, I'm…lonely. I…don't even know what time of the day or night it is."

The shadow, then sat cross-legged and placed its head in its hands, as if listening very carefully to her.

"Welcome to hell. Seeing we're both sharing the same cell, how about us becoming real friends?" She extended her right hand out. "Oh, but wait, I haven't even given you a name yet. Now, let me see…"

She thought hard, and then, snapped her fingers and said, hysterically, "It can only be Shadow Sheila!"

Just then, the main door burst open abruptly and two staff, a sharp-faced man in his mid-twenties, known as Meroni Stenson, and a short haired lady in her mid-forties, called Erica Bezotta entered her cell.

"Careful, Stenson," said Bezotta, wide-eyed.

"Yeah." He froze momentarily at the frail figure before him and her surroundings, then felt sickness in his gut at the sight of the blood around her face. Bezotta quickly grabbed the plate with a loaf of bread and a bowl of soup from his hands and placed it very quickly on the floor, not losing eye-contact with Sheila 'X' even for a second.

"I don't want your or anybody's pity! I just want out of here!"

This time, even Bezotta shook and they retreated backwards and reached for the cell door, but in that very instant, something uncanny happened: an eerie cracking sound broke the silence and the door abruptly slammed shut behind them, closely followed by a bolt that confirmed it was locked, which left them all in the pitch-black.

"Please, somebody open the door!" Stenson cried. "We're trapped inside!"

"Now you see how it feels? To be trapped inside a cell…with a she-wolf. Ha ha ha ha haa!"

"Now, we can have some real fun, all night long, hah hah hah hah hah! Howl! Howl Howl!"

"Listen, I don't know what game you're playing, Sheila 'X' but this could have very serious consequences, so you better let us out of here," said Bezotta. She dug into her uniform's left-side pocket and illuminated the room with a lighter.

No sooner had she lit it, when suddenly a pair of arms reached down through the ceiling and pulled Stenson upwards, throttling him until his body grew limp like a rag doll, then began to roast and sizzle until it turned into a heap of cinders that covered the floor, then faded away into oblivion. There was no trace of Stenson; as through he had never come. Sheila 'X' looked upwards, and grinned, then turned to Bezotta and gave a menacing snarl. Her eyebrows appeared thicker and had merged in the middle. Furthermore, she now appeared taller, as she stalked her around the cell, menacingly.

"Keep away from me. Keep away, or I'll." Suddenly, Sheila 'X' pounced upon her, forcing Bezotta to drop her lighter. This was followed by loud screams and the tearing of flesh.

In a short time, Bezotta's corpse lay on the blood-stained cell floor, after which, Sheila 'X' gazed up at the ceiling and whispered, "Thank you, Shadow Sheila. I feel a lot safer now with you."

There was no reply, no glow this time.

"I guess you must be sleepy." She yawned. "I think I'm going to turn in myself. But, boy, am I hungry." In reply, suddenly a plate of salad sandwiches and fresh fruit appeared through the wall before her, on a golden tray and rested on the floor. Her eyes lit up.

"Wow! Where were you, all this time? Now, I can kiss hunger goodbye! Thank you, Shadow Sheila."

As she took a bite, a thought entered her mind that maybe she could ask Shadow Sheila to help her escape, but only once she got to know her a little better. She yawned again, then curled up on the cold floor. Her eyes soon grew heavy and before long, she drifted into deep sleep.

The following day, in the mid-afternoon, she awoke to find herself lying on a long table, wearing a helmet and dressed in a straight-jacket, her hands and feet tied firmly, with electrodes protruding out.

A small team of nurses, of both genders, headed by Dr Ghoulder surrounded her. He approached her and said in a dry, croaky monotonous voice.

"Has anybody seen Stenson and Bezotta?" No response. Dr Ghoulder glanced at one of the team who stood by a machine.

"Give her a small shock." The assistant, a young Chinese man, named Yang Choo, reached for the voltage switch, and pressed.

"Aaahhhh!" His body ignited and burst into white-hot flames.

"Quick, someone put the fire out!" Shouted Dr Ghoulder, hysterically. But the moment he had said it, everyone froze helplessly, until a heap of ashes lay on the floor, which in turn, faded into nothingness, after which everyone found themselves able to move again and turned to one another in complete confusion.

Dr Ghoulder gazed at the empty space where the assistant had stood, then at the inpatient, furiously.

"You're responsible for this. I...I was wrong about you all along. I thought you were just another mentally ill patient, suffering from lycanthrope; but now, I realise you're some kind of a sorceress."

"Well, then you had better release me right away, or else, you'll all share the same fate."

"Are you actually *threatening me?*"

"No; I'm *warning you!*"

"Well, suppose I say you're bluffing? You know, I've never lost a poker game to date." His attention turned to the voltage machine and he reached for the button.

"If you value your life, don't do it."

Dr Ghoulder marched to the button and pressed it.

Suddenly, she felt the electricity enter her body, and she wriggled to and fro, screaming until smoke began to sizzle through her hair, palms, foot soles, mouth and ears. After this, she blacked out.

When she awoke, she found herself back inside her cell, in the pitch-black. Her body was still hurting and her eyes felt sore. She placed her hands across them and felt. There were swollen rings around them, due to the shock. Then, she recollected her thoughts and shouted out in the pitch-black,

"Hey! You betrayed me, in my hour of need. What were you thinking? I thought you were my friend, Shadow Sheila!"

In response, there was a cracking sound, reminiscent of something that had fallen from a great height. As she couldn't see anything, she felt the floor around her, until…

"Ewww. There's something wet lying here," she said to herself, feeling it. She brought it closer to her face and inhaled.

"Oh no; it's a decapitated human head!" At first, she instinctively tossed it to the ground, feeling repulsion. But this shortly changed to an eerie interest. Once again, she lifted it and decided to take a bite. Her teeth sank into the flesh of its cheekbone and she took a deep bite.

Just then, the door opened and Dr Ghoulder stood there.

"Choo's dead. You killer, I'm going to teach you a les…" His words drowned to a whisper and were cut short at the horrific scenario before him.

There she sat, holding a human skull, soaked in blood, stripping off pieces of flesh and chewing them.

"Mmm, this is delicious. Want to try some, Ghouli?"

His face turned pale at the sight and he felt like vomiting, but swallowed it in, then produced a syringe from his left-side coat pocket and to her surprise, he injected it into his forehead and began laughing manically.

"I know what you're thinking, Sheila Ashvernser, and no, you're not deluding; far from it."

"But…how did you know my name!"

"Oh, I've known all along. I'm physic."

"Psycho more like." She muttered. "I hate to ask, but I'm just curious to know, why on earth would the head of a psychiatric institute stab his forehead, of all places, and with a syringe?"

"Why would a young lady claiming she's not lost her sanity, drink human blood and tear off flesh from their skulls?"

She shrugged then tossed the skull to the floor and wiped the blood off from her lips, spitting out the flesh, some of which was wedged in her teeth.

"Never mind, I'm not interested, nor do I care, because now I'm going to reveal to you who I am, and more importantly, who *she* is."

Before she could respond, he stared up at the ceiling and pursed his lips then produced a high-pitched shriek.

In an instant, Shadow Sheila dropped to the floor, for the first time, standing in-between them.

It didn't end there. Dr Ghoulder's appearance began to change as well. First, his clothes dissolved off from his body. At first, he appeared stark naked, but then something strange began to occur.

He began to metamorphosise. Orange scales began to emerge through his flesh, all over his body. Then his tongue split into two and he began to hiss. His eyeballs turned a fiery red.

"The clue was in my name, you seeee…hssssss."

When he spoke, smoke seeped out his mouth.

"Let me explain...hssssss." Her eyes filled with terror and she turned in desperation to the door, but Shadow Sheila had now moved there.

"And here's the part you're really gonna relish, Ashvernser. Your friend and I have known each other for aeons...since childhood, in **hell**. Hah hah hah hah hah!"

"No, this is not happening!"

In desperation, she made a dash for the exit, to find her body set ablaze and burn into a heap of white-hot ashes, which disintegrated into nothingness...

The End.

Zuguh: Abomination from Hell!

Padre Wolfe, a frail high priest in his mid-nineties, was on the verge of closing his church door, when suddenly, a young lady came running towards him. Alarmed, he placed his frail hands over his face. She fell at his feet and held his legs, breaking down in a fit of tears. He removed his hands and looked down.

"My child, what is the matter? Please get up." He bent down and helped her up to her feet.

"Why are you in tears? Did someone hurt you?"

She fought back tears and spoke, "Padre Wolfe, only you can help me. I was expecting my baby but it was delivered dead. Now, my heart is broken. It's the third time and quite frankly…I'm inconsolable." She burst out in tears again.

"How tragic. I wish I could bring your baby back to life, but that power is in God's hands."

"I…I wish I was dead. Yes, now my life has no value. I'm going to commit suicide."

"No! Do not ever let this thought enter your mind again. It is the greatest and most unforgivable sin. Promise me!" He gave her a tight hug.

"I don't know what to do." She cried and cried, until Padre Wolfe's face lit up.

"I think I have the answer to your pain. But you will need to pass a test."

"Anything. Just name it."

"Follow me. Wait, what's your name?"

"Delilah Forester."

He held her right arm and led her through the church and out the back exit. There was a long narrow trail. It was pitch-black outside. Just then, he stopped and pointed at a mis-shaped fleshy lump lying by the gutter. It seemed to be making muffled crying sounds, almost in whimpers.

He approached it, then knelt down, lifted it and cradled it in his arms, humming a lullaby.

"W…what is it, Padre?" Delilah asked, bewildered.

"I've name it Zuguh. Behold, here is a child; your child."

"B…but what was it doing lying here? Is it even human?"

"It's a very long tale to tell. One night, as I had finished my sermon, I heard these strange whimpers as you hear now. After everyone had left, I discovered it. I dare not mention it to anyone, in case, they tried to harm it. I don't even know if its mother may turn up. If she *does*, I will inform her that her baby is being cared for by you. This is *your* test, Delilah; God be with you. Go now, and remember to hide it away and nurture it with love."

"Oh, thank you, Padre." And with those words, she covered the baby in her arms and rushed back home.

v

"Coochi-Coo. Coochi-Coochi! Now, I had better place you somewhere safe, Zuguh dear, before Terry comes home from work."

Delilah Forester swiftly carried off the baby into the kitchen and perched it on a chair. She then browsed through the cupboards until she found a box of Rusks. She plucked one out and handed it to the baby, just in time at the sound of the door-bell.

"Wait here, dear, I'll be back shortly." As she turned away, the baby's eyes rolled inside out and worms began to slide out from its sockets.

"Hello, Delilah." He placed his arms around her and gave her a tight hug and a passionate kiss.

"How was work today? Is Mr Forbes still harassing you?"

"No. If he was, then I wouldn't be feeling like dancing." Once again, he reached out to Delilah and began to waltz around the hallway with her. She suspected some good news.

"Oh, I think I understand. You got promoted, right?"

He released her and tutted.

"How on earth did you ever guess?"

"Body language, of course." Just then, there was a loud thud accompanied by crunching sounds. Both turned and looked at the kitchen door.

"What was that noise?" He asked.

"Wait here, I'll find out." She rushed inside and couldn't believe what she was seeing. There on the floor, the baby was crawling about, coated in blood. She panicked and turned around and banged into Terry, who was standing right behind her, in disbelieve and horror.

"What the hell is *that monstrosity*!"

"Oh, Terry! I'm so sorry. I was meaning to surprise you; not shock you; may I introduce to you, Baby Zuguh."

"Oh, no. Please don't tell me that uncanny creepy-crawly is a baby. Why, it's not even human, is it?" He approached closer and gazed at it.

"Delilah, please be honest with me. Where did you find it? And more importantly, what prompted you to bring it here? It looks so evil. I think it might be…a zombie."

"Oh, silly-billy. I found it lying abandoned by some garbage. I looked around and saw there was no one."

"So, you decided to pick it up and bring it home…" said Terry, frowning.

Upon hearing these words, Zuguh let out a pained cry and then began to crawl towards Terry's left leg.

"Aww, don't be so heartless, dear. It's only a child."

"I mean even you're referring to the gender of the baby as 'it'; I mean to say…"

Just then, Zuguh unexpectedly took a large deep bite into his leg and tore out a piece of flesh, then crawled back under the table and savoured it. Terry fell to the floor in extreme agony.

"Aaaahhh! Delilah, quickly, call an ambulance."

Delilah reached for the phone then paused. Internally, not a mother, she felt a maternal pull of protection towards the zombie-baby.

"Well; what are you waiting for?"

"No, there isn't time. I'll go and get my first-aid kit from the bathroom."

As she left, Terry's eye's stared in horror at Zuguh. He was genuinely petrified.

"I don't know who or what you are, Zuguh; but I can bet my life on it that you emerged from the gates of hell itself. I have no qualms with you. Please, leave us both in peace!"

Zuguh swallowed the flesh and began to giggle. Blood mixed with saliva dribbled down his mouth onto his dehydrated stark-naked dishevelled body. Terry could only gaze back in horror and confusion, until his head began to reel and then, darkness followed…

*****

"W…where am I?" Terry's eyes burst open and he found himself lying on a trolley-bed, covered with a white sheet and a name-tag attached to his right toe. He pulled it aside and looked around. He was in some freezing room, surrounded by corpses. Then, to his shock, one of them, a middle-aged lady, came alive. She had no eye balls, just black empty pits. She made a pathetic groaning sound with menacing tone to it. And then, she cradled her arms and walked right up to his bed.

"K…keep away from me. Keep away!" Terry stood up and staggered nervously to the nearest door.

"Help! Help!"

Suddenly, the zombie fell, lifeless once again, onto the floor, just as the locked door opened and one of the staff walked in, a man in his late thirties. He stared at Terry, wide-eyed.

"How did you…come to life? You were dead when we brought you in here."

"Oh, get out of my way!" Retorted Terry and stormed off, still in his hospital clothes.

Meanwhile, Delilah had a visitor. It was none other than Terry's boss, Mr Stephen Forbes.

"Sorry to bother you, Delilah. Is your husband in?"

"No. He was rushed to A and E yesterday, and declared dead upon arrival." She broke into tears.

"Delilah; there's something I need to tell you." Hardly had he opened his mouth, when Zuguh crawled into the hallway, from the kitchen, his mouth still dribbling with Terry's blood.

"Oh, my word! What is *that*?"

"Hey, don't talk that way about my Zuguh."

He knelt down to take a closer look.

"What's wrong with it? Is it a boy or a girl? It looks… demonic."

Just then, Zuguh began to rise into the air until it reached Mr Forbes' head. It came towards him then ripped his nose off his face. Mr Forbes screamed and fell on the ground, bleeding and screaming.

"Zuguh! That was really naughty." Zuguh giggled, chomping and enjoying its feast.

"Hmm, I wonder what he wanted to tell me."

*****

Later that night, Terry arrived back in the house and tiptoed in, wary that Zuguh could be anywhere in the house. He entered the bedroom to find Delilah curled up in bed with him.

"Delilah!" He whispered. He gently brushed his right hand on her legs. She awoke.

"You…you're alive!"

"Sshh! There's something I need to tell you, alone." She followed him into the hall and looked around, wondering where Mr Forbes had vanished.

"Yes, what is it, Terry dear?"

"I think I met Zuguh's mother at the Hospital Palliative Care Unit where the corpses are kept."

"And…?"

"She's one of the undead too. She wants Zuguh back, or else something terrible will happen…to you. She warned me."

"Terry, just listen to yourself."

"I know it sounds crazy, but I think Zuguh's real mother is going to take over your body, or turn you into one of the un-dead."

"Or Zuguh himself?" They turned to see Zuguh, who had transformed into a more humanoid figure. It had formed lips and its mouth opened, then it called out, "Maa Maa."

Its voice had an amphibious croak.

Almost instantaneously, a trail of smoke filled the hallway and through it emerged the same un-dead woman Terry had seen. She gazed at Zuguh, with a pitiful look and reached out to her child, but Delilah dashed forwards and lifted Zuguh in her arms.

"Don't you dare touch my Zuguh!"

Zuguh's mother let out a loud hiss and screamed. From her mouth, millions of maggots emerged and Terry appeared with a mallet and made a run towards Zuguh's mother. She turned to him, wide-eyed, and furious, then gazed at the mallet. It began to glow, hotter and hotter, and gelled onto Terry's arm, until he caught fire and was burnt alive. His skeleton lay on the floor then turned into a heap of ashes.

"Terry!" Delilah cried out.

"Give me back my child this instant, or else you will also die!" Her voice was a loud shrill.

"You don't scare me, you fiend. If you really loved Zuguh, then why on earth did you abandon her!?"

"Because she's not from our earth, my child: She's from the very gates of HELL itself!" Called out a familiar voice. Delilah swung around to find Padre Wolfe standing behind her. He held a pure silver cross in both hands and aimed it at the monstrous woman.

"Padre Wolfe, oh, I'm so pleased to see you, but how did you get in?"

"Fortunately, your main door was left open."

"Oh, Padre, what should I do?" He pointed to the trail of fire.

"This monstrosity," he said, pointing to Zuguh's mother, "it walks on flames. These flames, begin from the gates of Hell. And now I have to make a painful decision." He gazed at both the women and then stroked Zuguh.

"What decision?" Delilah asked, bewildered. "And what about this test you mentioned earlier?"

"Oh, you have passed my test in flying colours. You have proved that you love Zuguh more than her. She had tossed it down from Hell, so it crashed into the gutter, at the back of my church. On humanitarian basis, I decided to raise it. It was just a tiny ball of flesh, but it made sounds, and it was alive. I was not sure what to make of it. Was it good, was it evil? I had no idea." There was a long thoughtful pause, then he continued. "I could easily have reported it and have it taken away, but I would never have forgiven myself. You see…it was a question of morals." Tears trickled down his eyes and he gazed up. "Lord, if I have done a sin to protect and raise this fellow mortal, who does not look, act or behave like us humans, then please forgive me." He took a deep sigh, then composed himself and stared at Zuguh's mother.

"What is your name, oh evil and callous demoness?"

"Bhooparrah." She replied, in the same high-shrilled croaked voice.

Delilah cut in.

"Be careful of her, Padre, she's now one of the un-dead. Terry told me she was actually a dead body in the palliative sedation ward."

He looked at both Delilah and Bhooparrah. Then said, "Well, if neither of you can decide who the child rightfully belongs to, then I shall."

And then, he snapped his fingers and called out at the main door.

"You can come on in now, Woolum, and do your dance of death." They all gazed at the door as a giant dark burly man of ten feet tall, with coloured paint all over his body, emerged and began to strange uncanny tribal dance. He also sang out loudly and kept stamping his large feet on the ground. Each time he did so, Zuguh's mother temporarily began to fade. As he quickened his pace and danced faster and faster, she looked at him, helplessly. And then, in a split-second, she made one great leap forwards and grabbed Zuguh and then both vanished. Delilah had just managed to blink her eyes and react to what had happened. Woolum stopped his act and stood behind Padre Wolfe.

"It is done."

"Thank you, Woolum, you may leave now." He bowed his head and left. Padre Wolfe turned to Delilah.

"I'm so sorry about your husband, Terry. May his soul rest in peace."

"And what about my Zuguh?" She asked.

"Take comfort in the fact that you have passed the Lord's test and proven that you look for good even in the most evil and callous monstrosities. Now, rest assured, God will have a beautiful award awaiting you, perhaps in the form of a new life partner and perhaps even, a little child of your very own. The Lord works in mysterious ways, Delilah, my child."

"Thanks, Padre Wolfe. I will definitely now attend your sermons more regularly. One more final question."

"Ask away, my child."

"Who was Woolum?"

"Perhaps an angel come to help us?" He winked and smiled, then added, "Take good care of yourself; only good things come to good people like you. Goodnight and God bless you."

The End.

The Deceased Cubicle of Succubus

Someone or *something* was lurking about, amidst the thick blanket of smog that concealed the damp marshland. It had picked up the scent of a teenager camper soon after he had stepped out the warmth of the B&B named The Goblet of Blood, into the cold, dark moonless night, equipped with just his backpack and a torch. At first, he was completely oblivious to the danger and continued across the trail, but at the sound of heavy breathing closing in on him, he instinctively spun around and whispered, wide-eyed, "Who is it? Who's there?"

A moment's silence was suddenly followed by nervous whimpering sounds that echoed all around him. He panicked, dropped the torch then ran as fast as his feet could carry him. Assuming it was a wild animal, he stopped, unbuckled his backpack, containing a lunch box, and tossed it aside, hoping it would deter it. He paused to catch his breath, then waited, but in a few moments, a loud chilling howl filled the air and it was at a very close range. In a frenzy, he continued to run, until he stumbled and fell on the damp ground. Loud snarls filled the air and then something lashed out and ripped a chunk of flesh from his right leg, after which he rolled across the ground in agony and fell into a deep and dark pit. Darkness followed…

*****

When he finally regained consciousness, he found himself lying semi-clad in a white garment in a foetal pose, unable to move, in what appeared to be a glowing yellow cubicle. After what seemed eternity, he heard approaching footsteps after which one side of the cubicle slid open to reveal a tall slender yellow-robed figure who held a tray in her hands containing a glass of water and a plate of food which she placed on the floor beside him, but he could only express himself through his eyes.

She sensed what he was trying to say, then approached him and touched him softly with her finger tips which felt cold and like jelly, then left the room before she could say a word.

He stood up, relieved, and flexed his body and noticed that his wound had healed up completely. Just then, the cubicle slid open again, but this time from the opposite side, a tall slender beautiful young lady appeared, barefoot and clad in a transparent pink silk gown. Her hair was auburn and flowed down to her shoulders. But most distinctive were her green eyeballs with piercing yellow pupils.

"How are you feeling right now?" She asked, in a seductive purring voice.

"M…much better, thank you; but where am I, how did I get here and, who are you!?"

"Oh, you ask so many questions."

"All you need to know right now is that you fell in a pit, developed a concussion and were, very fortunately, I may add, rescued by one of my helpers. And now, you're in my custody." She giggled.

"Well, you're very kind…"

"Layeeya."

"That's an unusually pretty name. Thank you, Layeeya, for saving my life, but now I must leave."

He looked around at the surrounding cubicle walls, which then turned black.

"Multi-coloured cubicle, eh. Very cool. Now, which is the way out?"

She gestured ahead and he smiled. But as he attempted to walk, he felt nauseous then fell forwards onto the floor. Layeeya licked her lips, walked up to him, then placed her left foot on his injured right leg. He felt a jabbing sensation and noticed she had sharp retractable talons at the ends of her feet, while her hands were webbed.

"You're still weak…at least spend the night here, Ferth…" She purred.

"How did you know my name?" He said, wide-eyed.

"Oh, I know *everything* about you." She snapped her fingers and one side of the cubicle slid open and the same yellow robed helper appeared.

"I've temporarily paralysed his legs. Help me place him over there." She pointed in one corner.

They lifted him like a rag doll then place him on the floor.

"Now, Ferth, it's time for you to dream and meet Succubus."

"Succubus?"

"She is our high priestess, the linin-demon queen, Mortella. For many years, she has sought out a young male, such as yourself."

"Hah hah hah hah hah!"

"I...I don't understand." Layeeya knelt over him, then bit some venom into the left side of his neck, in the jugular vein, after which he fell unconscious.

*****

When he regained consciousness, Ferth found himself lying in an enchanted forest.

"Well, at least I'm outside that darn cubicle," he said to himself, "I was starting to feel claustrophobic."

"Now, all I need to do is find out where on earth am I?" He stared down at his right leg and realised his wound had healed completely. However, the bite marks on the left side of his neck were still stinging.

"Maybe, Laayeeya poisoned me and I've woken in some dream world."

In that same instant, the sound of an irresistible lullaby filled the air. It was mesmerising and overpowering.

"What a beautiful voice. I have to find out who the singer is." It echoed all around him, so he wasn't sure and pondered which direction to go. Suddenly, the singing stopped abruptly and turned into a frenzy scream, filled with terror. This was shortly followed by a loud chilling howl, similar to the one he had heard earlier in the forest.

"Oh, no! Someone's in trouble." He ran ahead swiftly through the trees, deeper and deeper into the forest, until he reached the scene.

Ferth's eyes widened in horror at the sight before him. There on the ground lay blood-soaked dismembered body parts, scattered around. Some were suspended from tree branches. They appeared to belong to some lady, perhaps the same one who was singing. Among them, he saw a large pair of white wings, ruthlessly shred. She had been mauled and torn alive, and whoever, or whatever did it, was not very far away. And then, there was a nervous, uncanny whimpering sound, followed by heavy breathing; someone was approaching. Ferth looked around to find a place to hide, but it was too late. From out of the forest, the 'beast' appeared for the first time and showed him its putrid face. It closed in and began to circle him, intimidatingly, after its hairs stood on end. Ferth stood frozen. It snarled and then pounced on him. He covered his face with his left arm.

"Aaarrrggghhh!"

*****

"Woe woe! Our Queen Mortella is no more!" Ferth found himself lying back inside the cubicle. It was pitch black and Laayeeya stood over him, her face cupped and in tears.

"Hey, I'm really sorry, but I was nearly killed myself!"
"Some hideous beast pounced on me. I was a sure gonner, I can tell you."

Laayeeya cried hysterically. She was inconsolable.

"E…even the cubicle walls have turned a pitch black. It has deceased. Now, we are all doomed."

Ferth began to feel sad himself. He sat up and placed his arms around her.

"I don't understand what you meant."

"The cubicle was active and could travel through space and time. It was a living organic spacecraft which communicated with us, through its use of colours; it was...our guide and friend. Now, we are stranded here on *your* planet."

Ferth couldn't resist laughing.

"Hah hah hah hah hah! That's the most absurd thing I've ever heard."

Laayeeya pulled herself away and stepped back, infuriated.

"How dare you mock my words? I speak the truth. You are a just a mere mortal, where as *we* are an advanced race, The Avellons, from the future. Come back again."

"Hey, no problem. That's what I want! Now if you could be kind enough to show me the way out, I will be happy to."

Laayeeya turned to one side of the cubicle and stared hard at it. After a few moments, she tried again. She turned to Ferth, then stared around her.

"It's all your fault."

"No, it's not the boy's fault." They both turned. It was the tall yellow robed figure. She walked up to Laayeeya.

"If you permit it, then I can explain to Ferth what has happened."

Layeeya nodded.

"Thank you." She then turned to Ferth. "When our queen, Mortella was slaughtered by that hideous beast, not only was our spacecraft destroyed, but the skin tissue that makes up this cubicle as well."

"Hey, wait a minute. I recognise you, but we haven't been formally introduced yet."

"I'm Tamaata-07."

"That's a peculiar name, but then, I guess you're also an Avellon."

"When you were transported into the forest, at the same moment, our Queen Mortella was brutally slaughtered by the beast. Now, our scanners showed that there are no such beasts around here, so…"

"So, you want me to go back there and slay the supposed beast? Well, I am flattered you see me as some kind of heroic vanquisher of monsters, but I'm not cut out for that kind of thing. Now, I will take your leave."

"Oh well, I tried my best, and we can't force you to help us."

"Now, will you please let me out!"

"As I mentioned earlier," said Laayeeya, "it's *no longer* functioning."

Ferth turned around and gazed at all four sides of the cubicle. They were indeed dark. Even the droning sound had stopped. It felt as if the essence of its being was no more. He turned back to Layeeya and Tamaata-07. Both had tears in their eyes. It was then that he had a change of mind.

"No strings attached? Alright; I agree to help you, but on one condition; that you let me walk away free after that."

"Agreed!" Both called out at once. "But first we need to 'prepare' you with a costume and ammunition."

The End.

Where the Qori Ismaris Abides

Trapped inside the cold black walls of the cubicle, Ferth was suddenly struck by a jolt in the back of his neck, then blacked out and was whisked through time and space. Only this time, when he regained consciousness, he found himself lying again a forest in broad daylight, fully-clad in a shining golden armour-plated suit. There was even a glowing large silver and platinum sword and shield that rested on his chest. As he stood up, he held up his armoury and noticed upon closer inspection, there were large diamond-shaped mirrors around the border of his shield. But what really caught him by surprise was the sight he saw when he gazed seemingly at his own reflection. Momentarily, he did not recognise himself. His face had matured and hardened. It was the beautiful chiselled face of a hero, with carved cheeks and dark brown eyes. And then, he heard the voice. It sounded familiar.

"Go now, Ferth. We have evolved you to your full potential. Now, you are grown up. Be our redeemer and save our cubicle by avenging our slain queen. Seek out the beast and return back to us, victorious. Good luck!"

"Layeeya?" The voice echoed and faded away into oblivion. As Ferth took his first steps, he found more power in his joints. He was able to move effortlessly and had developed muscles.

He smirked and said to himself, "There's no disputing that the Avellons had planned this all along."

He had barely uttered these words when a loud cackling sound filled the air, followed by a menacing snarl. Instinctively, he tightened his grip on his sword and shield, then spun around, ready for combat. There was no one in sight. Only the sound of the whistling wind that blew against his cheeks.

"I know you are stalking me, fiend! Why don't you come on out in the open and fight me. I challenge you!" No response. Just pin-drop silence.

"Bah! Just as I suspected; a coward. Well, I'm not afraid, and I'm going to seek you out and slay you. You hear me?" Ferth continued walking through the dense forest. Along the way, he noticed there were fertile cranberry trees. In fact, there were so many berries that they stooped down. He gently plucked off a few and was about the taste them when he felt a frail bony hand on his right shoulder.

"I wouldn't eat that if I were you, young man, it's toxic."

He turned around swiftly. A semi-clad skinny old man stood before him, holding a long stick in his right hand.

"Thanks, but who are you?" Ferth asked.

"My name is Keynadiid." He took a bow.

"I am Ferth. But could you tell me, where exactly am I?"

He burst out in a fit of laughter, then looked at him quizzically.

"My, dear friend, surely you must be knowing this is Somalia."

"And why are you dressed in that…unusual costume?"

"Even if I told you, you would never believe me."

"I apologise. It is none of my business. Will you care to walk with me to my humble abode and be my guest for the night?"

"Seeing as it's just the two of us, how can I refuse such hospitality. Thank you for your kindness."

Keynadiid laughed out and began to rub the stick vigorously against his flesh. Ferth raised his eyebrows, but he kept quiet at his strange gesture. He figured that perhaps he had some skin problem.

"We had better quicken our pace, Ferth. It will be dark soon." Ferth stopped in his tracks.

"What is it?"

"Cut the crap. I know who you are. No more games."

"I beg your pardon?"

"When I appeared here, I heard a cackling sound, followed by a menacing snarl."

"You mean...you also heard it?"

Ferth pulled out his sword and pointed it at Keynadiid's throat.

"I'm warning you."

"Does the name Qori Ismaris ring any bells?"

"You talk in riddles. Explain yourself!"

"The Were-Hyena, according to our medieval bestiary."

"What?" Just then, it dawned on Ferth that the stranger might be telling the truth. Or perhaps, he was playing mind games. In any case, he decided to play along. He watched as, once again, Keynadiid rubbed the stick against his flesh. Arms, chest then legs.

"Are you feeling alright?"

"Why do you keep doing that! It's so annoying to watch."

"Look, you must believe me. We have to reach my place before nightfall. No matter how well armed you are, the beast is far too powerful and mighty. It will devour both of us unless we make a move now!"

"Then how come you survived so long, Keynadiid?"

There was a prolonged silence after which he walked right up to Ferth's face and whispered, "I'm totally petrified and a coward, so I hid."

"Alright, lead the way."

Up above, dark clouds were moving in. Soon, the full moon would be out. There was little time to think and enough to act…

As they treaded through the forest, it began to rain heavily. The bare trees projected the appearance of uncanny menacing figures reaching out to grab and devour anybody passing by.

Just then, Keynadiid who was walking ahead of Ferth stopped in his tracks and turned to face him.

"Why don't we just pitch camp right here?" He planted his stick in the damp earth.

"And get soaked? Thanks, but no thanks. I don't want my armour all rusted up. Come on, let's just carry on. It can't be that far."

"But I want to rest here!" Cried out Keynadiid, in a loud and high-pitched sound.

Ferth's face froze as it dawned on him that Keynadiid was not who he appeared to be. And then again, he drew out his sword, then waited and watched in pure shock and horror as the bony and frail figure before him began to sprout hairs and grow physically larger and larger, taking on the form of a giant golden-brown and white spotted abomination; a were-hyena to be precise, better known to locals as the Quori Ismaris. It stood upright, on its hind legs, measuring at least twenty-seven feet and gazed down at the puny Ferth, with its protruding yellow and purple eye balls, drooling from its immense jaws, then let out a maniacal giggle, reminiscent of a human being.

Ferth wasted no time and raised his sword to strike, but the moment the sword made 'contact' with the mythological beast, it suddenly vanished into thin air and then it began to snow heavily.

Seconds later, a familiar multi-coloured object began to materialise again out of thin air. It was the cubicle of Succubus. The front side slide down and out emerged two figures. He recognised them instantly.

"Layeeya! Tamaata-07! Oh, I'm so pleased to see you. But what became of the Quori Ismaris?"

"It was just a figment of your imagination," replied Layeeya. "We conjured it up to test your wits and heroics."

"A test if you like," added Tamaata-07, "to make a man of you."

"But what of your beloved Queen Mortella?"

In response, they both turned and looked back at the open door of the cubicle, as a slender tall lady emerged, dressed in a mustard robe. And she wore a golden crown with red rubies.

Layeeya made a gesture for him to take a bow. Ferth instinctively knelt down as Queen Mortella approached him, then discarded his sword and tapped his left and right shoulder.

"Rise, Sir Ferth, White Knight of the Avellons."

"Your Majesty, I'm truly honoured, but what of my youth? I appear to have leapt forwards in time."

"So, you now desire to leave us and return back to that point in time before you entered the cubicle?"

"Well, if you put it that way, I do."

"So be it. Now, you have surpassed the test we set for you, it is our duty and honour to uphold your wish."

"Your Majesty, forgive me, but we cannot let him leave before we have had prepare our main course," called out Tamaata-07.

"Thank you, ladies, for your hospitality, but I…"

Just then, to Ferth's bewilderment, all his armour vanished, including his sword and shield, after which his hands began to tremble and his face felt a strange sensation. He was changing back to the same teenager.

"Hey, what's going on?"

It didn't end there. Layeeya walked up to him and bit deeply into his jugular vein, hissing. He froze in his tracks, felt a numbness, then crashed to the ground. Layeeya let out a loud giggle, as did Tamaata-07, kneeling down at their prey. Their mouths began to drool over Ferth's body, coating it with their saliva. And in a short while, Queen Mortella approached them and flexed her jaws then called out, aloud, "Oh, Keynadiid! Din-din is served!"

A moment's silence followed, after which, to Ferth's horror, the Qori Ismaris re-appeared from the dense forestry, cackling out aloud and then pounced on its prey, instantaneously tearing out its heart and devouring it in one morsel.

The End.

"Blood Blood"

It was nearing sunrise and in her laboratory, at her work desk, Dr Lizzie Helfern, a frail but attractive botanist in her late sixties, sat transfixed on her stool, peering into the eye-piece of her microscope at a shredded filament of a tree root. As she increased the magnification to its optimal level, her eyes widened in dismay at the sight of blood emerging from it. Intrigued, she momentarily sat up and gently rubbed her eyes with a handkerchief from her upper coat pocket, then continued inspecting it. Only this time, what she saw terrified the daylights out of her. Before her eyes, strange sinister symbols were forming in what appeared to be human blood.

"Henson! Come over her, quickly!"

Within moments, the sound of rushing footsteps could be heard and a young robust man in his early twenties barged in.

"What is it, Dr Helfern? Is everything okay?"

"Quickly, take a look at this." She stood up and moved across the door biting her nails anxiously.

Henson gazed into the eyepiece and his head rolled back. He turned and looked at her.

"No, it can't be possible."

"What? Please explain it to me."

"Do you know what these are?"

"Well, you're the only translator that works on these premises. Please enlighten me."

"These symbols are Ancient Egyptian Hieroglyphics. I think I can translate them too." He produced a notebook from his left-hand side pocket and drew out the ten symbols.

"Now, pull over a stool and let me explain. First tell me precisely what exactly do you see."

She stared at them pensively.

"A leg, a lion, two birds and a hand. Then again. You've done it twice, mistakenly."

"No, that's because it *reads* twice." She pushed her hands through her hair and gasped.

"I still don't know what it reads, Henson!"

"Alright, if you're not too busy, Dr Helfern, why don't you pull up a chair? I'd like to give you a very brief history lesson, if I may?"

"Go ahead, I'm all ears."

"Well, firstly, let's just get our heads straightened out and place all superstition to one side and focus on the facts."

"The original Ancient Egyptian language was used in AD 391, in the reign of the Byzantine Emperor known as Theodosius, but when he declared that all pagan temples to be permanently closed, his orders led to a four-thousand-year tradition, including their language being vanished for at least 1500 years."

"Go on."

"Fortunately, upon the discovery of the Rosetta stone and the work of a Jean-Francis Champollion, they saw sense and revived it in the form as we know it today. So, what we have here is a form of Ancient Egyptian Hieroglyphic writing which dates back four-thousand years Before Christ, and coincidentally, they also had a decimal system up to a million. I just thought I'd throw that in to tickle your brain-buds." He smirked.

"It...it means that 'whoever' or 'whatever' wrote out this message must be an Ancient Egyptian spirit."

"Hey, slow down, Dr Helfern. Let's not be too hasty and jump to conclusions. After all, they were a literate lot; and it must be emphasised that they hailed their hieroglyphics as, and I quote, 'the words of God.' Isn't that amazing?"

"Well, thanks for the history lesson, Henson, but it concludes me to ask, what does it spell out?"

"Blood Blood."

Upon uttering those words, she noticed Henson's eyes vanish and replaced by two blood-soaked empty sockets. Not only that, he was dressed as an Ancient Egyptian warrior with a long golden head-gear and held a golden staff. His feet were bare and he wore sandals.

"Aaahhh!" Suddenly, in a flash, he appeared normal again, and looked at her, surprised.

"What is it now? Did I say something to upset you?"

"Y...you changed your appearance and your eyes were just two empty blood-soaked holes."

"What?" She sat down on the stool and broke down.

"Hey, I'm sorry. Maybe I came across too strong. Listen, I need to find out the tree where this mysterious bark came from. Any ideas?"

"Jubokko," called out a voice. He turned to the door where a tall, lean, dark-haired Japanese man stood, with a long moustache and slanted eyes. He wore a traditional conical Sugekasa cap, with yellow and magenta strands running down the back, some of which fell across both his shoulders and was dressed in an elaborate silvery-gold gown with colourful designs "Say, who let this wizard get in here? I hope you realise that these are private premises!"

"My humble apologies for the intrusion, but I have come to warn you that both your lives are in grave danger and only I can help you. That particular sample you are researching has been extracted from an ancient cursed Japanese tree known as the Jubokko. It drinks human blood."

"What balderdash!" said Henson. "I hope you realise that my colleague is already deeply distressed. Security, get this lunatic out of here!"

"No, hold on," said Dr Helfern, rising from her stool. She walked right up to him. "How do you know all this?"

"It has been foretold by our ancestors that one day, the cursed pharaoh, 'Blood Blood' will rise from his grave and seek vengeance on all his persecutors. That day of reckoning has now come."

In the meantime, two security guards appeared.

"There is no need for that. I came of my own accord and shall leave of my own accord. Here is my card, should you require my services." He pulled out a red card from his right inner sleeve and handed it to Henson, after which he swiftly clapped his hands and vanished in a puff of smoke, in front of them.

"Holy smoke! I was right after all; he *was* a wizard."

"This is no time for wit and humour, Henson, we need to think what our next move is going to be."

"Right. I'm with you all the way, Dr Helfern." He then turned to the security guards and tapped his nose, then whispered to them, "Err, don't mention this to anyone, but we're actually on a secret mission, working undercover, so you can both go back to your duties, thanks."

The bewildered security guards left, confused and scratching their heads.

Meanwhile, elsewhere at a nearby estuary, a strange skeletal figure with sockets for eyes lumbered out from the shallow pit of a river. It was covered in slime and its intestines were clearly visible. As it walked, it turned its head to and fro, hissing and sticking out its long slimy tongue, on the lookout and ready to lash out at human victims, then suck them inside it.

Meanwhile, back inside her laboratory, Dr Helfern and Henson were studying the red card left by the unannounced mysterious visitor.

"What a strange name," quipped Dr Helfern, "Ulzado."

"Hate to say I told you so, but I *did* tell you he was a wizard. Don't you just hate being right all the time." Henson knew that Dr Helfern was close to a mental breakdown, so was trying to lighten the atmosphere. But then, a bright glow filled the air and his body grew stiff and rose in the air, almost touching the roof.

"Sorry to barge in on your research, Dr Helfern, but I wanted to break some good news. I have just unleashed the Mohrg, one of my three chosen monsters to seek out and destroy my persecutors. So get them; before they get *you!* Hah hah hah!"

In the spur of the moment, Henson's body changed to the same Egyptian figure, then back again. He fell to the floor like a rag doll. Dr Helfern rushed to his aid.

"W…what happened?" He rubbed his right hand through his hair as she helped him to his feet.

"Y...you were possessed by 'Blood Blood' and we're in deep trouble. He mentioned a creature called the Mohrg. Can you shed any light on who or what it is?"

Henson's eyes widened in horror.

"Oh, my God. I need to act fast!" He rushed to the door.

"Where are you going?"

"There's no time to explain. Just trust me. Oh, and in the meantime, get all the security guards to keep a lookout on the premises. If *it* appears, blast it to smithereens."

"Wait! What exactly does it look like?"

He stared at her and replied.

"You'll know when you see it." And he left.

Dr Helfern made an announcement to security, after which she decided to take matters in her own hands.

"I can't just sit here and twiddle my thumbs. I have to do something. If this monstrosity is something supernatural, then ammunition won't affect it." She looked around her room desperately in a bid to find something that could hold it back, or stop it.

Outside, at a cemetery, an enormous casket mysteriously appeared and creaked open. It was filled with blood, out of which emerged another monstrosity. A bloodied and blackened giant figure. It had supernatural strength and took leaps, looking upwards at the darkening sky. Just then, it was spotted by a grave digger.

"Oih, who's there?"

The gravedigger headed in its direction, and within seconds, the monstrosity leapt over him and rested on his shoulders, then dug its deep talons into his skull and squeezed out all his blood.

"Aaaahhh!" It drank the blood with its sharp long canine teeth, then headed instinctively forwards.

Back inside her laboratory, Dr Helfern had gathered some bottles of acid and harmful bacteria when suddenly, she heard a scraping sound at the window. She turned to look and her eyes grew wide in fear. Words were being formed in blood.

"Draugr. It must be the second of the three monstrosities. I must warn Henson; but where on earth could he be?"

She grabbed hold of two of the acid bottles and headed for the door which instantly slammed shut. She reeled backwards and the bottles fell and smashed on the ground, spilling the acid.

"Damn it!" She then turned the door handle, but it did not budge, after which she banged on the door and yelled at the top of her voice.

"Help! Security! Is anybody there?"

"Henson, where are you when I need you the most?"

Her eyes fell on her work-desk, where the red card rested.

"I'm not sure if it's wise to summon that weirdo, but on the other hand, it's a chance I have to take. I don't stand a chance against 'Blood Blood' on my own. Maybe he can help me fight him."

But just as she walked up to it, a sudden chilling breeze blew it off, onto the floor.

But this was no ordinary breeze. It was in fact the breath of 'Blood Blood' blowing it away, out of her reach.

"I know it's you, creep!" said Dr Helfern, gazing up at the air. "Well, it is going to take a lot more than that to stop me. For some reason, you're afraid of me calling your friend; or should I say, enemy!"

She made a sudden leap to the floor, caught it and tried to recite his name, but the card was blank.

"Damn it! What now!" In desperation, she rubbed it, like a magic lamp and then, in a flash, the same wizard appeared. He raised an eyebrow, smiled then took a bow.

"May I applaud you on your wisdom, Dr Lizzie Helfern?"

"We're in deep trouble. I need your help. That creep has unleashed some monstrosities. They're out there right now, as I speak! Don't you even have a name?"

"Calm down, please. I am a wizard, that is all you need to know."

"Is there anything else I should know about 'Blood Blood'?"

"He was once a good man, but great injustice fell upon him. He was to be crowned the new pharaoh, but the reigning pharaoh was jealous of his popularity and ordered his guards to execute him in such a manner that he would be completely forgotten, as if he never existed."

"Firstly, he was caught in the middle of the night and his tongue was plucked out, then he was held forcibly and the name 'Blood Blood' was branded across his forehead; then he was thrown alive into a deep pit of poisonous snakes and buried. There, a Jubakko tree was planted, so no one ever suspected his body was underneath it. Ever since, his restless spirit roamed about, seeking vengeance on his persecutors."

"I almost feel sorry for him," replied Dr Helfern. Then, her eyes lit up.

"Of course! It means that the only way to destroy him is to de-root that tree and…"

"Better still, I have to cast a spell to exorcise 'Blood Blood' out from it. The tree is ancient and feeds on the blood of innocent passers-by to sustain his 'life' after which it will instantly dehydrate and die."

"Great. So, when can we begin?"

"Right away."

The wizard then moved to a clear space in the room and sat cross-legged on the floor.

"What is the precise time?"

Dr Helfern looked at the wrist watch on her left arm.

"Five fifty-seven pm."

"Perfect. Now, listen very carefully, as there isn't much time left, I am about to perform an ancient spell to make contact with Amaterasu, sister of Susanoo, the God of storms and the sea and of Tsukuyomi, God of the moon and must not be disturbed *at any cost*. It has to be performed at *precisely* sunset. You may witness things that astound you; for instance, I will be lending my vision to the goddess and in the process, various colours of the rainbow will filter through my eye sockets; do not be alarmed by what you witness."

"Wow. I'm speechless. And I give you my word, I promise. In fact, I'll leave the room."

"Wait, Dr Helfern! There is one other thing. There is a chance, as the goddess is using my body as a tool, there is a very likely chance that I may also perish, so in that instance, I will say thank you for trusting me and goodbye."

Dr Helfern shrugged.

"You know, it's strange. We only just met and I don't even know your name."

It had now reached 6 pm and without a reply, the wizard began his mantra and began to hum out aloud and chant some ancient Japanese words. For a moment, Dr Helfern stood, transfixed, then slowly made her way out the room.

"This may be the right time to look for Henson."

As she made her way through the outskirts of the plant-gardens, she noticed two sizzled corpses lying sprawled out on the grass. Upon closer inspection, she identified them to be the left-over remains of the security guards "Ewww! Eugghh!" She carried on vigilantly, but unarmed, with only her will to survive.

Suddenly, she heard a loud thud, as if something had landed from a great height. This was shortly followed by another sound of smashing glass. She looked upwards at the glass enclosure ceiling. Her heartbeat was rapid and she was perspiring. At that instant, she knew she was not alone. She crouched down and temporarily hid under one of the large plants, to catch a glimpse. Nothing in sight and just pin-drop silence.

As Dr Helfern shuffled forwards, heading for the nearest exit, she felt something slimy under her boots, like glue. She looked downwards and noticed peculiar black blobs. Then, a trickling sound followed and then, a menacing hiss.

"Aaaahhhh!" She spun round and saw her persecutor. A large frightening figure of immense proportions loomed in the air; a combination of ghost, zombie and vampire, namely, the Draugr. The un-dead, malicious fiend's skin was blackened, bloodied and scarred from previous battles and encounters and its expression was of sheer hatred and revenge. Worst of all, it had spotted her, and she was his next victim. It glided downwards and flexed its jaws to tear her to pieces when it was distracted by a menacing hiss. It looked forward, with its dark, eyes, dripping with tears of blood. Dr Helfern also looked around, shuddering.

On the opposite side, facing them, was another un-dead fiend. This one was a skeleton, the same one which had emerged from the river-bank, namely, the Mohrg. It was absolutely repulsive, with its intestines clearly visible and dangling out from its rib-cage. It also had an unusually large dark blood-red tongue, reminiscent of a snake, that was protruding out its jaws.

"I'm dead meat!" cried out Dr Helfern. "Oh, well, I might as well make a run from these monstrosities. At least I can die with my dignity intact." Suddenly, she made a dash forward and found herself being hunted down. As they reached out to grab her, there was a dispute between them, as predators do over their prey in the form of a feeding frenzy.

Dr Helfern could not believe what she was seeing. They had both turned on one another.

She looked up into the air and smiled.

"Someone up there definitely loves me."

Just then, in a flash, they both vanished into thin air. This was followed by a bright flash, followed by thunder and rain.

"Sorry, Helfern, I guess it's just not your day today. I'd better head back to my laboratory."

She opened the door to find the room empty. She looked around, but the wizard was nowhere to be seen.

"Where did he go?"

She sat down on her stool, and looked up in the air, and again thanked the stars for giving her what was literally a new life. But then she remembered something.

"Damn it." She spoke to herself. "But what became of the biggest fiend of all 'Blood Blood?' If he's still out there, then he could unleash more monstrosities, then all of mankind will be in danger! Henson!"

And then, a bright ray filled the space where the wizard had sat and a distant echoed female voice filled the air.

"Do not be afraid, child. I am Amaterasu, the Japanese Sun-Goddess. I have come to you as you are pure-hearted and to inform you that the wizard's prayers were successful. Do not be saddened, as he was a great soul and he is now in a place where all good souls abide. He sacrificed his life to save yours."

"I feel honoured, great and wise, Goddess." She bowed her head respectfully. "But what of 'Blood Blood'?"

"I have vanquished his insane evil spirit from the cursed Jubakko tree where he lived all these years. He is now forever in the fiery pits of hell."

"One more question…"

"I know what you are going to ask me, my child. Behold, and goodbye."

The bright ray vanished and Henson suddenly appeared at the door.
"Henson! Boy, am I glad to see you!" She ran up to him and gave him a tight hug.
"Where on earth were you?"
"Relax. Actually, I travelled back to the time of the Pharoes and met 'Blood Blood'. I'll tell you all about it later."

He smiled to reveal a set of decayed yellow teeth, after which, his eyes momentarily turned a bright scarlet-red; just like those of 'Blood Blood'.

The End.

And Now for My Next Trick

Dominic 'The Gifted' Prance, a young and upcoming magician was performing one of his live shows at a club in East London in front of a small audience and he was determined to win them over. A stage had been set up especially for him. As the red curtains slowly rose upwards, the audience held their breaths in anticipation. There was nobody there. Suddenly, there was a very loud bang and a thick blanket of green mist began to engulf the entire stage, followed by sparks and crackles.

Slowly but surely, a tall slim man emerged. In appearance, he was smartly dressed in a black Victorian suit, red and black laced cloak, top hat and polished black boots. His hair was dyed Prussian blue with yellow ochre side burns and tied back tightly and ended in a long pirate cut knot. He also carried an Egyptian magic wand in his right hand; rumoured to be the only existing one of its kind. He looked around at his spectators and then took a swift bow. This was followed by loud noises from the audience.

"Well, when are you going to show us your bunny rabbit then?" An elderly lady shouted, who burst out coughing and laughing, poking her snoring husband's left side. On another side of the club, a bear of a bearded man said in a husky voice, "Oih! Listen up, people, I bet he's now going to pull out a handkerchief or a deck of cards. Just you all watch and see. It's all the same. Rubbish. Boo! Bring on the pole dancers!"

Before long, the entire place was in a shambles as they all joined in and called out, raising their fists in protest and stamping their feet on the floor.

"Boo, go back home! Boo, go back home! Boo, go back home!"

Before long, the club owner, Mr Collins approached Dominic.

"See, I told you, didn't I? They're just not your type. They're used to seeing the likes of Can Can dancers or pole strippers and what have you."

Dominic Prance turned to him and raised both his arms in the air. Suddenly, he blew softly at Mr Collins. But what he blew was not just air; it was red glitter and before he could react, Mr Collins began to rise in the air.

Higher and higher he rose, until his head touched the roof of the club in front of the surprised audience.

"Now, you just stay up there until I finish my act, thank you very much." Dominic then turned to the audience and focused his attention on the same lady who had remarked about the bunny rabbit. She gaped in surprise and whispered to her husband, "He's good, George. Blimey, I was wrong about him, I was."

"My, good lady, would you please come on the stage for a moment?" At this point the audience were completely quiet and curious that what is going to happen next.

"Can you dance, my good lady?"

"No, I've never danced in my life. And I'm not your good lady. My name is Peggy Hart."

"Ladies and gentlemen, for the first time, this lady, sorry, I mean Peggy, is going to perform the Irish jig at bionic speed. Behold!" Dominic produced an Egyptian magic wand and waved it at her. Suddenly, Peggy began to do the Irish jig. Faster and faster she danced at lightning speed. Dominic waved his wand and she rose in the air and turned upside down, doing jigs in the air. He then raised his hands at a young man in the crowd who began whistling jingle bells through his nose.

"I hope you are all having a good time, my dear audience. And please do not attempt these tricks at home, good people." He then snapped his fingers and all the people in the front row began to flap their arms like birds taking off.

"Now, what else can I do?" Dominic said to himself. "Ah, yes. And now for my next trick!" He waved his wand at the back audience and they all stood up and formed a line, like a human train, and began to kick their legs in and out doing the Cha Cha Cha. They moved around the club. Dominic smiled and took a bow.

"Well, I hope you all enjoyed my show. As you can see, there were no rabbits, no handkerchiefs nor any deck of cards! And now, I think I will take my leave and hopefully, the next time you see a magician, you will all think twice and show a little respect and courtesy. Oh, and I nearly forgot something." He turned to the bearded man and waved his arms up. Suddenly, the man's beard was filled with cement which dried up all over and he grew a set of deer antlers on his head.

"Oh, and before I take my leave, rest assured, the effect of my spells will wear off in precisely nine hours. Good day."

He took a bow and left.

The End.

'Cutting Down'

"Come closer; closer, closer," whispered the fading voice, after which the blurred image of a frail female skeletal figure slowly appeared, dressed in a yellow transparent robe. But just as it reached out a bony hand, the distinct tone of the alarm clock sounded and Karen Catherson's eyes burst open. She sprung upwards, and found herself in bed, sweating from her nightmare. Her heart was still beating fast. She rushed barefoot to the full-length lipstick mirror that rested at an angle in one corner of her bedroom, to take a good look at herself. "Uggh!" she said, pinching some skin around her waist. "Still too much flab for my liking. I still need to cut down some more." She then slid out the weighing machine from under her bed and stood on it.

"63.5 kg!" Infuriated, she moved across the room and switched off the light, then collapsed back on her bed, fatigued and starving. In the background, the radio had been left running and was playing some debate about losing weight.

"Well, all you calorie-counters out there, remember not to go to bed hungry. Sleep tight, until the same time next week, good night."

"Go suck an egg!" She protested, and as if in response, the radio channel closed down and there was pin-drop silence.

*****

The following morning, Karen had overslept, then realised she had an appointment at hospital for a consultation with her dietician. She panicked as she rushed to get dressed. Within half an hour, without even a sip of water, she left home and caught the first bus. When she arrived, she went to reception and apologised, after which she sat and waited. Before long, she was called by a nurse who escorted her to a door and left. Karen knocked softly and then entered. A smart middle-aged man suited and booted, wearing glasses, sat behind a desk and stood up to greet her, but his smile faded at the sight of her. He composed himself then said, "Miss Catherson?"

"Y…yes."

"Please be seated." He gestured to the chair beside her, opposite his desk. He then turned to his computer and pressed a few keys to bring her medical record on the screen.

"You've been diagnosed with Pan Colitis for a considerable number of years. How are your bowels?"

"Not as they should be functioning."

"Any bleeding?" She nodded.

"About two teaspoons of blood since last month. And I haven't been eating since."

"That's not good. Food is essential to sustain life."

"But when I was eating, I couldn't keep it down and I just kept vomiting."

"You never feel hungry?"

"All the time, but I just can't keep it down. Besides, gotta cut down on those calories!"

"Hmm." The dietician's face dropped and he spoke in a low deliberate tone.

"Your colitis appears to have worsened by this flare up and I'm afraid one of its symptoms is anorexia nervosa."

"W…what is that?"

"It's an eating disorder which occurs when the disease is at its severest."

"Damn, so what am I supposed to do about it?"

"You need to overcome your fear of food. Convince your mind that eating is normal and natural."

*****

Karen Catherson had spent most of the afternoon in the washroom of Reggie's Bluebird Restaurant. And now it was late evening. When finally, the door clicked open, she emerged, feeling weak and faint, then walked wearily to the table where her date, Bernard Harrison, had been waiting. He was gazing at his watch repeatedly and was not happy.

"Karen, you look so pale. Do you realise you've been in the washroom for nearly two hours! At one point, I nearly walked out. I mean what on earth were you doing in there?"

"Well, if you *must* know, I was bleeding away; it's colitis!"

"What?"

"Listen to me, Bernard; we're in a restaurant and I *don't* feel comfortable discussing any of my health problems in here or anywhere, come to think of it!"

"I'm sorry, dear," said Bernard, placing his hands affectionately onto hers. She moved them away.

"It's alright, but I'm warning you, that if you try that again, then I'll leave." Bernard stared back into her eyes and said softly,

"I won't."

"Good. Now, I'd like to go home to my apartment." Karen stood up.

*****

Later that evening, upon reaching Karen's one bedroom flat, Bernard parked his car just outside the door. He stared at her.

"Would you mind if I walked you to the door?"

"No, thanks. I can manage."

"No need to be so formal, Karen, you're my date for the evening, remember?" He said, reaching out his hands and caressing her left shoulder. Karen smiled nervously and opened her side of the door, then without a word, made her way back into her flat. Bernard shrugged and drove off.

Once inside, Karen kicked off her shoes and headed straight to her bedroom where she pulled out the weighing machine from under her bed.

"Sixty kgs."

"You're not trying hard enough, Karen," said a ghostly voice. Karen spun around abruptly and got a shock. There inside the mirror, stood the same ghostly apparition who had called out to her in her nightmare. A frail skeletal lady, uncannily resembling her, and dressed in a transparent yellow robe. Karen backed away and rubbed her eyes in disbelief.

"No, you can't be real. This is just my imagination, playing tricks on me."

"Oh I'm just as real as you are. Only thing is...I'm trapped inside this darn thing." Karen looked around helplessly and ran to leave the room, but the door slammed shut.

"Ah ah aah," said the apparition, waving a bony finger. *"Did you know that the human skeleton consists of 206 bones, six of which are the tiny bones of the middle ear? That's three in each ear, which function the hearing."*

Karen closed her eyes tightly, hoping it was all a nightmare then re-opened them slowly, but the thin, emaciated figure was still there.

"W...who, or what on earth, are you?"

The figure burst out laughing, her voice echoing across every corner of the room. Karen crouched to the floor and cupped her face.

"There's no need to be afraid of me, Karen. I'm your twin sister, and you can call me Kaye. Now, I can look into your mind and see there is some attraction to your date. But there's one thing he ain't tellin' you. Wanna know? He thinks you're too fat for him, and that's where I come in. I can help you cut down to just the right size."

"H...how could you possibly help me? You're just a figment of my imagination and I refuse to believe you're real." In response, there was a bright glow and in the apparition's hand, a small green shimmering box instantly appeared, which she tossed in Karen's direction. It came through the mirror and fell on the floor at Karen's feet. Bewildered, she lifted it.

"They're laxatives; and they're real!"

Karen looked back at the mirror, but the apparition was gone. Everything was back to normal again. She opened the box which contained some tablets. Something compelled her to take one, which she swallowed then turned out the lights and collapsed to the comfort of her bed.

*****

The following morning, the alarm sounded at 8 am, followed by a click, after which the radio turned on automatically to *The Calorie Counter Hour*.

"Wake up, all you lazy bones, out there and let's get those calories burning! On today's show, we're going to discuss the benefits of jogging. That's right, listeners, I said J-O-G-G-I-N-G. Now, we need to get that metabolic rate to rise sooo..."

"Go leg it!" said Karen, and turned it off,

"Actually, that's not such a bad idea." She got up, feeling light, and put on her tracksuit and headed to the door, on an empty stomach. There was a letter marked 'Urgent' on the floor. She lifted it and tore it open. It was a follow-up appointment at the dietician tomorrow afternoon.

"Great. That's all I need."

Karen opened the door, locked it then went for her morning jog. Outside, it was a bright and sunny day. But barely had she taken the left turning towards the park when she suddenly felt an uncontrollable painful urge in her stomach, realising the laxative Kaye had given her must have started taking its effect. Back in the washroom, she literally burst, halfway through the door and a trail of blood, accompanied by mucus, trickled all over her dress and onto the floor. It didn't end there. She fell on her knees and vomited.

"Eugghh!" This whole trauma lasted for half an hour. When she finally got the strength to rise to her feet, Karen stood up wearily and staggered through the hallway and into her room to the mirror, closing the door from behind. She held her stomach, still in pain and weighed herself. The expression on her face changed and she smiled gleefully.

"38.1!" She removed all her clothing and stood before the mirror, stark naked. But in an instant, the apparition appeared and she backed away, shocked and embarrassed.

"Hi, Sexy."

"Look, please just go away. Leave me alone!"

"That's not a nice way to talk to your twin sister, is it? Especially when I'm helpin' you get fully prepared for Bernard."

"Yeah, I suppose you're right. Do you think I look sexy; Kaye?" The apparition nodded sideways.

"You're gettin' there, but there's still too much fat on you. But, not to worry. Just take another of those laxatives I gave you. This time, take two."

Before Karen could reply, the apparition smirked and vanished from the mirror.

"Kaye's right, these laxatives are just what I needed!" Without hesitating, she reached for the box of laxatives which lay under her pillow, took another tablet out and swallowed. Within a few moments, she felt her stomach churn and then she rushed to the washroom.

*****

The following morning, Karen found herself lying crumpled on the floor in a pool of blood. Her body felt cold and damp. When she looked down at her clothing, she realised they too were drenched in blood. As she tried to stand on her feet, she felt sick, and vomited in the sink. With sheer will power, she got dressed but found her clothes were so loose, she had to fasten a belt around her waist. In a short while, she left home and made her way to the dietician, by bus.

'*Why is everyone staring at me*,' she wondered, '*like I'm some kind of clown.*' Before long, when she finally arrived, she walked weakly inside the dietician's room. But when his eyes fell upon her, he looked at her horrified.

"A…re you the same Miss Karen Katherson?"

Karen smiled and replied, "Yes, but why do you look so surprised.?"

"What have you done!" She blushed.

"Well, you tell me. How do I look?" She stood up and twirled around then sat down.

"Have you not looked at yourself in the mirror lately?"

"Well, to be honest, I was in a rush this morning, so I didn't look, nor did I weigh myself."

"Listen to me. I don't know what you're doing to yourself, but please stop it right now." Karen looked bewildered, then stood up and left.

"If that's all, I need to leave now. I'm expecting some visitor. Have a nice day, Mr…Say, I didn't even read your name on the letter!"

"It's Mr John Curwins. Here, come and stand in front of my mirror." He stood up to assist her, but she managed to shuffle to her feet and walked up to it.

"Well, what do you see?"

"Eeuggh. Still could lose some more weight."

"Miss Katherson, for goodness' sake. You're a living breathing skeleton! Your symptoms of colitis have made you anorexic and unless you start to eat and drink, quite frankly, this may well be our last meeting. I don't know what you do in your private life, but please look after yourself, or I will have to contact someone to forcibly…" Karen had heard enough and left the room, slamming the door, frowning.

"He's probably just envious of my body and looks."

*****

Back home, Karen rushed to the comfort of her bedroom and slid out the weighing machine from under her bed.

"Wow! 31.751 kilograms!"

In a state of ecstasy, she made a leap to the mirror but upon doing so, felt a sudden snap in her arms and legs then fell crashing to the floor.

Within seconds, the full mirror filled with the image of Kaye. She looked across the room at Karen's body and with delicate ease, stepped out, and into her room.

"Bernard Harrison, here I come!"
The End.

Zom-Bait

Distress signals from an un-identified beacon in outer space had caused panic and excitement for the small crew of three aboard space-shuttle Vanya-14. This, in turn, had prompted the Command Pilot, Commander Vanya to make a split-second decision to respond right away. She was an attractive young lady, with a blonde perm that flowed down to her shoulders. Seated at the helm, she turned to her science officer, a man in his forties who stood to her right.

"Anything further to report, Bailiff?"

"I'm afraid not, Commander Vanya. But only once we reach the beacon, then we can begin our investigation."

"I figured. What I meant to say was…" Suddenly, the lights began flickering and then, darkness.

This was shortly followed by a magnetic thrust and a very loud clamping sound, followed by an eerie silence.

"Everyone stay in your positions, until I say." Commander Vanya leant to her left side of her chair until she felt a button. She pressed it and a small compartment opened. She pulled out an oil-lamp and a box of matches which she kept for emergencies such as this. With delicate precision, she struck a match and lit it. Within seconds, the deck was illuminated.

"At least we can all see where we are now."

"Carter, if you can hear me, you have permission to activate the generator."

"But, Commander, I can't."

"That's an order."

"I don't do impossible ones, Commander."

"Explain."

"Well, because the fuel cells used to operate it require one crucial component of the power system."

"Get to the point, Carter!"

"Alright, at its simplest, they require the electrical power system. You see, the fuel power plants generate heat and water as by-products of electrical power generation."

"Alright, Carter, that's enough. I don't need a lecture."

"Commander Vanya," called a high-pitched voice from behind. It belonged to Llanya, the Scientific Adviser, who was also second-in-command.

"I would like to make a suggestion. Seeing that we don't know who or what is on the other side of that door, it might be a good idea to send in the robo-scanner, just to make sure all is safe and clear."

"Brilliant, go ahead, Llanya, How long will it take?"

"A full scan of the beacon? Well, judging by its sheer scale, I would estimate a couple of hours. It's a health and safety rule."

"I understand, but we can't really do much, just sitting in a pitch-black shuttle. Can you program the robo-scanner to work its way in a mode so it works in conjunction with us?"

A beam of enlightenment spread across Llanya's face and she nodded.

"Yes, Commander Vanya, considering the circumstances, that might be the best approach."

Commander Vanya smiled and winked at her, reassuringly.

*****

Upon reaching the exit door which was linked to the beacon, they were surprised to see it glide open. It was almost as if they were being invited inside. But where were the occupants?

Robo-scanner glided along the floor, bleeping continuously and the small crew of four proceeded with great caution. In a short while, by the time they reached the end of the corridor, they found themselves struggling to breathe as toxic fumes began to seep out through filters on the surrounding walls. A stench of decaying bodies filled the air and then the floor beneath them gave the illusion of moving from left to right, as cracks and splits formed. Furthermore, robo-scanner began to overheat and evaporated in a matter of seconds.

Suddenly, everything grew still. They looked at each other, with a mixture of intrigue and fear, guessing what may have caused it. Somehow, it had not occurred to any of them to bring along any ammunition. And when it did, it was already too late to turn back. They were entering the unknown. Commander Vanya broke the silence and said, "It's becoming more of a puzzle."

"What next, Commander?" Llanya asked.

"We split into two groups. Llanya, go left and take Carter with you. Bailiff, you come alone with me. We'll meet back here at this point in approximately thirty minutes, got it? Okay, let's make a move."

No sooner had Llanya and Carter disappeared down the corridor when there was a very loud yell and the sound of hurried footsteps.

"Commander Vany," called out Carter, wide-eyed and hysterical. He was huffing as he spoke.

"Quick! You *have* to see this." They followed in his footsteps down the left corridor until they reached a bloodied door. It gilded open and inside was the most revolting sight they had ever witnessed. Even Commander Vanya trembled, but composed herself.

"Decomposed bodies rows upon rows of them."

"Commander, maybe whoever sent that distress signal was under attack and ended up like one of these."

"Under attack by whom?" Carter asked. Both stared at Commander Vanya.

"What do we do now, Commander?" Carter asked.

"I'm thinking, Carter, I'm thinking!" Suddenly, she turned around, then faced Carter, furiously,

"Where's Llanya?"

"I...I don't know, Commander. She was looking around and seems to have vanished."

"You idiot! I can't trust you even for a few moments! Come on, let's find her."

"There's no need," called a voice from the back. They turned.

"Llanya, thank goodness, you're safe," said Commander Vanya.

Llanya smirked and said in a soft voice, "Oh, you need not worry about me. I may be safe, but you're certainly not."

"Llanya, are you out of your mind?" Commander Vanya said.

"I've never felt better. This is *my* moment, *my* time." She gazed at the decayed bodies which were poised in compartments, lined in rows across the room.

"I can't believe I'm hearing all this," said Commander Vanya.

"Ever since I joined the federation, I've envied you; but now the tables are about to turn. Watch."

Llanya pulled out a long knife from her left side pocket and in one swift move, sliced across her wrist and laughed manically as the drops of blood fell onto the floor. She retreated backwards and pressed the door button.

"Before you leave us in this dilemma, just tell me who it was that sent that signal."

"Moi," she replied, pointing her bloodied arm to her bust.

"You're crazy!" said Carter.

"Yes," she said, with a manic grin. "I suppose I am."

"But why did you bring us all the way here?" Commander Vanya said. "If you had issues with me, we could easily have sorted out our differences in private."

"No! I hated you so much. I wanted to corner you and bring you here. You see, this beacon once belonged to me and my crew."

"That's sick," said Bailiff.

"One more word out of you and…"

"Oh, well, I guess it makes no difference anymore. You're all my Zom-bait. At least, that's what I prefer to call it."

"That's silly, everyone knows zombies are just all made up. You're just trying to scare us."

"Alright then. Everything I said was trash. Now, why don't you take a look over *there?*" They turned to their right.

"No! It can't be possible. It...it's actually moving," said Carter. "We have to get out of here."

"Llanya, your rivalry is with me. Let my crew go free."

"You're so skinny, your flesh won't even fill up one of them. They're all hungry and haven't eaten for centuries. Your deaths will be very slow and agonising as they prefer to eat live bait, I mean to say...Zom-bait! Good riddance. Hah hah hah hah hah!"

"No, please don't leave us here to die," cried Commander Vanya.

"Oh, I was saving the best for last. Here's the twist; you won't die. Upon their first bite, you're literally one of them. Goodbye, suckers."

Llanya left, locking the door from outside by which time the zombies were all active and moving around. At first, they instinctively began to lick the blood stains off the floor, which soon turned into a manic frenzy, after which they stood up and crowded around the three of them and then the sharp sound of ripping flesh and crunching bones, followed by screams of unbearable and agonising pain.

"Aaaahhhhrrrggg!"

The End.

Clown Cemetery

It was the dead of night, in freezing winter; minus 35 below zero to be precise, as the old banger took a turn and crashed straight into a gravestone with a sinister looking clown engraved on it. Strangely enough, below, were some words that read: *"Isn't it just hilarious being dead?"*

Intrigued, the driver, a man in his late seventies stepped out to investigate. Somehow, he was not too bothered, let alone aware, that his vehicle had stopped dead and he was trapped in a large burial ground. He coughed and placed his glasses on, then gazed around. His eyes could see row upon row of seemingly endless gravestones; and all had a mixed variety of clowns with messages below them.

"How odd," he said, then decided to move forwards to kill time and read another, then another then another, until he came across one that made him freeze.

"Welcome to Clown Cemetery, Martin Perther. RIP."

"W…who's responsible for this sick joke?" He swayed his body, left and right. Just then, he heard a loud honk, followed by another and another. It was coming from his car. Martin rushed to look inside, to find a large blue honker attached under the steering wheel.

"That wasn't there before." He wiped his brow and tried to retain his composure, fearing his sanity.

"It's useless trying to start you," he said, looking at the car. "There seems to be only one way left. I have to walk through this cemetery and find the nearest station." And so, he turned around and began walking straight ahead, past the gravestones.

His feet felt unusually heavy shortly afterwards, and he found himself plodding. Then, he looked down and was horrified to find that he had on a pair of long red clown boots with yellow laces. Martin leant downwards and attempted to pry them off, but to no avail.

"Darn. These are glued to my feet! What am I supposed to do now?" At that same instant, a pair of white laced gloves appeared on his hands. Once again, he tried pulling them off, but they were firmly sealed onto his flesh.

"What in the heaven's name is happening to me? All I need now is a clown costume and a red nose!" Then, in a flash, that also happened, coupled with a tiny black top-hat. He began to laugh manically.

"It's a nightmare, yes, it must be. Perhaps there's a clue to all this on those etched gravestones. Now, all I need to do is to tediously read through them all!"

As he proceeded further, attempting to read some of the faded ones that came his way, he heard whispers. They appeared to belong to a young female. He strained his eyes in the misty sky, then noticed a lean figure kneeling down on one of the gravestones. In excitement, he called out aloud, but as he tried to do so, he burst uncontrollably into a fit of hysterical laughter.

"Hah hah hah hah hah hah hah!"

Martin clenched his fist in frustration, tears rolling down his cheeks. Even they felt different. He felt his face with both hands and noticed there was a black and white paint across his entire skin. Despite this, the figure turned towards him and walked up to him. She held a doll which she cradled gently in her arms.

"Oh, you must be one of the newbies. My name is Floenza. Who are you?"

"M…Martin. Martin Perther."

"Enjoying reading the gravestones? They're fun at the start, but wherever you decide to roam, don't even think of going to the dark tomb at the far end of the cemetery. If you do, you're finished."

"Well, it's not as if I came here by choice, Floenza. At least you didn't change into a clown. Just look at *me*! Ha ha ha ha haa!"

Just then, she vanished into thin air.

"Hey. Where did you go? Oh, well, when you got to go, you got to go!" His face froze. He had not intended to make a joke of it. Some supernatural power had taken over his body and mind. It was becoming more apparent every moment that some evil presence was around.

"Perhaps it's some kind of a riddle. If I solve it, then there's a remote possibility I can be free of this. All I can do right now is to take Floenza's advice. I'll read through the gravestones."

The ground beneath his feet was damp, soggy grass. As he continued, a pair of green hands with long yellow claws suddenly burst out the damp earth and grabbed both his legs, tugging him downwards. Martin's eyes widened in terror and he tried to pull himself free. He fell to the ground, kicking his legs to and fro, until the hands let go then disappeared back into the earth. He then heard a voice call out,

"You can run, but you can't hide from us. There is no escape from the Clown Cemetery; hah hah hah hah hah!"

Martin painfully got up, out of breath with the struggle. It was a near-death experience for him and he was grateful to be alive. He continued moving through the cemetery, reading the gravestones.

"Maureen Kessle-RIP 1722 to 1749. Nothing sinister about this one."

He heard a roar of thunder, then felt a droplet of water fall on is cheek, then another and another. It had started to rain.

"That's all I needed. I think I need to head back to my 'clown car' for shelter!"

"There's no turning back now, Martin Perther, only forwards," called out an eerie spectre's voice from beyond the grave. "Just a little while left now, before the end of your life. Hah hah hah hah hah!"

"Not if I can help it. I'll fight you with every breath in my body…with the one thing I still have left." He reached up to his neck and held out a shimmering silver and platinum crucifix. There was no response. Just pin-drop silence.

"Help me, please," called out a pleading voice from a nearby gravestone. "Help Help!"

Martin looked around desperately then spotted what appeared to be a priest, whose body was half submerged in the ground.

"Hold on. I'm coming to help you out!" Martin rushed to the priest and was horrified to see that his face appeared to be rotting. His skin was shredded and some of it was hanging down his face. He also had bloody sockets instead of eyes. But most scary of all was the inside of his gaping mouth which was oozing out slimy snakes and a yellow and green puss as he spoke.

"Please, you've just got to get me out of here. I...I don't want to die."

Martin reached out both his hands, but then retreated.

"Aaahhrrgg!" He cried in pain and held his head, shaking it to and fro. Something uncanny was happening in his own brain. New thoughts were taking over and they were ones of a dark nature. It was a metamorphosis. Then, without a second thought, he raised his left leg up and with all his might, stamped on the priest's head, squashing it into a bloody pulp, after which he laughed manically.

"Hah hah hah hah hah!" He then knelt and ripped the head off the priest's body, decapitating it and took a deep bite from it, like munching an apple. When he'd had enough, he dropped it to the ground and kicked it into orbit then wiped then blood off his lips with his left hand and proceeded further down the Clown Cemetery.

"Marin Perther! Now, there's only one-way outta here. I challenge you to a showdown!" An un-human voice boomed out and it was coming from the same dark tomb at the cemetery, which Floenza had warned him about.

"Who, or what are you?" Retorted Martin. "Reveal yourself. I accept your challenge who, or whatever you are. I will prove to you that *there is no greater evil than I.*" There then followed a long silence, after which the voice replied.

"Yes, the time has finally arrived for me to reveal myself: after all, it was *I* who brought you here, you stupid buffoon! You see, once I have my victims where I want them, namely here, then, I first like to toy with them, after which I change them according to their inner nature. That is why I changed you into a clown, spiced up with some of my very own evil."

"I see. Well, what is the reward for the winner of this duel, may I ask?"

"Whatever you wish for. In one snap of your fingers, you will get anything you want."

"Even my own life back to what I was before coming to your clown crematorium?"

"Yes. But you're not going to come out of here alive because…no one has *ever* fought and won against…"

Suddenly, the temperature dropped very rapidly to minus 50. After this, the entire crematorium evaporated into thin air and changed into a dense freezing forest. Then, there followed a spell-blinding flash.

"Come and find me, sucker," hissed out a loud voice to Martin Perther, or what had become of him.

He looked around at his new surroundings. The voice seemed to be coming from all directions, so he decided to move forwards, looking in all directions.

"Boo!"

The figure revealed itself. There before him, stood an extremely tall, cadaverous, and haggard being with a yellowed, decayed skin, coupled with rotting eyes. It appeared very undernourished and hungry, as it stared down at the puny figure of a clown before him. His stomach rumbled out aloud.

"I'm so hungry. I haven't eaten in a long long time."

"What in blazes are you?"

"I am known by mankind, as a Wendigo. I have the power to change my unfortunate victims into anything I please. Now your time has come. There is no turning back, Martin Perther. Prepare to meet your death!"

Martin made a desperate attempt to leap forwards, but his feet were glued to the ground. Slowly and steadily, he lost all sensation of his arms and legs which grew numb. The Wendigo had paralysed him and let out a loud roar of manic laughter.

"Hah ha ha ha haa! Now, I can enjoy my latest feast."

He heard those last words as the Wendigo closed in on him and tore him limb by limb, eating him alive. In just a few moments, a pile of bones lay on the ground, drenched in a pool of fresh warm blood.

The End.

Beware of the Wendigos!

"You ask me who I am; well, let me introduce myself, by cluing you in…"

"I, and my kind, are those terrifying creatures of the night who prey on those unfortunate victims that dare to venture too far from their kind, by luring them away by imitating human voices. I especially enjoy stalking lone hunters in the dead of night, when it is snowing heavily and await once they are completely blanketed and they freeze; that is when I strike. I am as tall as a tree, and when my victim sees my ghastly appearance, as tall as a tree, they freeze in terror as I gaze and laugh at their helplessness, then stare down with my coal hot eyes, then proceed to sink my razor-sharp teeth into their tender flesh, after which I let out a loud blood-curdling loud triumphant scream."

"They know me and my kind as Wendigos, and we are the dark spirits of hunger and famine. BEWARE OF US ALL!"

The End

Hafhogr Egod AD

"Hey, Asvoria, come and look at this!" called out Aegir. The middle-aged couple, both Norwegians, were outdoors in a dense forest to be precise, with hand luggage, backpacks and spades, on a 'holiday trip'. They were searching for 'relics', belonging to Bigfoot. She made her way hurriedly, towards him.

"What are you doing in that pit, Aegir?" She responded, with a bemused look across her face. "Come out of there. This is no time for fun and games."

"Asvoria, this is not a prank; and please show some respect for our heritage. Don't forget, we are North Germanic."

"Yes, yes, also known as Ascomanni; but instead of giving me this historical lecture, you still haven't explained why you are in that pit."

"It's *not a* pit. It's a giant foot belonging to none other than Bigfoot!"

Asvoria rubbed her eyes and walked slowly around it, glancing rubbing her chin.

"Hmm, you *might* just be right this time." As if in reply, a thunderous roar sounded.

"Quick! Help me out of here, before it comes back!"

She knelt down and reached out her arms and carefully hauled him out the footprint.

"How on *earth* did you fall inside in the first place?" Asvoria cried, panicking.

"I didn't look where I was going. It just appeared, like a dip, and next thing I found myself sliding down." Once again, the loud roar sounded and they decided to make a run for it, in the opposite direction.

"Aegir, where are we going?"

"There's bound to be a B&B a couple of yards ahead for tourists. We'll stop there for the night, then continue our quest at the crack of dawn."

A short distance behind them, the stamping of heavy feet could be heard, heading in their direction, followed by yet another ferocious roar. They quickened their pace.

Suddenly, a very tall and burly figure appeared out of nowhere. He waved his arms up and down, as if signalling, or perhaps even warning them to stop. When they didn't, he blocked their path and stared down at them, infuriated.

"Stop!"

They froze in their tracks before him.

"C...could he be...?" Asvoria asked Aegir. Just then, the giant burst out in a fit of laughter.

"I am known by the name of Eotin, but you may call me Ettin."

"That's Anglo-Saxon!" quipped Aegir.

"Correct."

"Why, that's also an ogre's name, if I'm not mistaken," added Asvoria.

"Who are you? And why are you both here. Have you no fear of Bigfoot?"

"I am Aegir and this lovely lady is my wife, Asvoria."

"Can't say I'm pleased to meet you. Now, as you are my guests, I ask you to accompany me to my abode. It's a short distance from here, through the forest and a stretch of river. Come, do not fear me."

Aegir glanced across at Asvoria, nervously. She gave a shrug and as they turned and began to follow Ettin, a large log landed just behind them.

"Hafhogr Egod!" called out Ettin and in a second, lifted them both over his shoulders, like rag dolls, and lumbered forwards at full speed.

Sometime later, they arrived at a cottage. Ettin placed the couple carefully on the ground and wiped his forehead with his left forearm.

"Consider yourselves very lucky to be alive."

Just then, the cottage door opened and a large female ogre emerged.

"Ettin! You have finally brought some guests with you; and after a such long time!"

"Allow me to introduce my wife, Assay."

"We thank you for saving our lives and for your hospitality," said Asvoria, "but we can only spend the night here. Tomorrow, we need to continue on our quest to find and bring back evidence of Bigfoot."

Ettin gazed into her eyes, infuriated.

"After all you've just been through? Why must you insist on finding evidence? Some things are best left…a mystery."

Assay ushered the couple to a table and seated them.

"Now, wait here. Soup will be served shortly."

"Please, make yourselves at home. I'm just going out for a walk," said Ettin.

The moment he left, Aegir turned to Asvoria and whispered.

"I can't help thinking we're being held here against our will."

"Don't be so paranoid, Aegir. We were both there at the scene. You saw what happened."

"Hmm, perhaps you're right. It's been a very long and traumatic day; let's try and get some sleep."

Outside, there was a full moon. Its glow fell across the cottage onto their faces.

The following day began with a chattering noise, accompanied by squeaks. Asvoria was the first to awaken and she felt something clamped on her neck.

"Eugeehh! G…get off me! Someone helps me!" She had to use both her arms to pry it off.

The second bat was across Aegir's neck and he appeared to be in a coma. No response.

Just then, Assay entered the room and began to hum a lullaby to which the bats responded and flew off, out from the nearest window. She then opened one of the side cabinet drawers and brought out some antiseptic and a roll of bandages. She gasped to get her breath back and then turned to Aegir and shook him. He flopped across the bed and fell off onto the floor.

"Oh no! Is he?"

Assay knelt on the floor and felt his wrist. After this, her head bowed and she nodded.

"I…I'm so sorry, he is no more." She then attended to Asvoria with her medical kit.

"Y…you planned all this, didn't you? Even the bats responded to your lullaby."

"You are wrong. I can assure you these bats are a common visitor here. I tried all kinds of methods to lure them away, but they keep returning."

Just then, the door barged open and Ettin entered.

"No sign of your Bigfoot!"

Asvoria broke down in tears. Assay shushed him and pointed to the bed where the bloody body of Aegir lay, his head slumped sideways and blood-drops trickling onto the floor.

"Oh no. I'm sure it was those bats again. Damn."

Asvoria wiped her eyes dry and looked around desperately.

"I need a shovel."

"What for, dear?" Assay queried.

"To give my husband a decent burial…and after that, I'm leaving."

"But where will you go? What about your Bigfoot?"

"To hell with Bigfoot, or Hafhogr Egod AD, whatever you folk call him. My life is meaningless now."

"Is it *really*?" Ettin replied. "It was your husband's mission to take back with you some evidence. If you allow us, we can help provide that evidence. But first, we need to use Aegir's body as a bait to lure Halhogr Egod here. Do you agree?"

Ettin turned to Assay and gave a wry grin and winked. He then produced a large syringe from his left side coat pocket and advanced towards Aegir.

"I will need to give you a dose of this first. Oh, do not be afraid. It's merely a sedation to calm you down."

"No, I won't take it. I think I'll leave now."

"But you cannot leave your beloved Aegir like that, for the bats, surely," said Assay. Their tone had changed now to a more menacing and intimidating one. They advanced closer and closer to Asvoria.

"No…no, keep away from me."

They both started to laugh hysterically at their helpless bait.

"Or else?" They both called out, simultaneously. The echoes of their laughter filled the air.

"One *final* warning to you both to keep away from me!"

This time, both made a dash towards her.

Suddenly, the ground beneath their feet began to shake until cracks appeared. Ettin and his wife Assay were taken by surprise and the vibrations made them come crashing to the ground. But it did not end there. To their shock, Asvoria began to metamorphosis as her entire body began to grow larger and larger. Hair began to sprout from everywhere until she was literally unrecognisable. The cottage smashed to the ground as she grew so large that even the tree-tops appeared like tiny plants around her.

"You, puny, devious foolish people. Did you really think for a moment that you could expose me to the world? All this time, it was *I* who was stalking *you!*"

Ettin and Assay turned to each other, completely taken back and tried to make a run to safety, but it was too late. With delicate precision, Hafhogr Egod knelt down and clasped his right hand around them and lifted them up to his lips, then licked his lips and devoured them in one swallow. He then looked into the forest and called out.

"Be warned, strangers. If *anyone* ventures out to expose my existence, then they will *all* share a similar fate. Some tales are best left, untold."

The End.

Brass Mineral Lighthouse Hospice for the Terminally 'Undead'

A towering Brass Mineral Lighthouse Hospice for the Terminally 'Un-dead' had been painstakingly built in hell, using zombie-workers, by order of the Federation of Monsters, whose presiding member was none other than Beelzebub. It stood planted in the red sea of blood, with its blinding beam of light. The in-patients, all monsters of course, had been brought in by the Grim Reaper on his raft of human bones, which acted as their ambulance across the vast bubbling hot seas of blood. The reason for this being that, quite recently, out of nowhere, a 'deadly' pandemic had appeared and was spreading fast, infecting the monster population. This 'infection' had no name yet, not a cure. Only one thing was for certain; once it was caught, it made its victims more...*human,* announcing that the end was near. Only one mineral-brass, kept it at bay, for a short while. The 'infection' also affected each kind of monster differently.

Inside the lighthouse, an endless row of spiral stairs led to various corridors that in turn led to wardrooms where monster-patients were being cared for. There was a 'secluded ward' where final end of life care was provided by staff, namely, under palliative care and palliative sedation.

Inside one of the upper wards, a 347-year-old lady-ghoul stood and looked around with her with her blood red eyes, drooling saliva wherever she walked.

"Would anyone fancy some nutrition?" She asked, in a pained croaky voice. She held a brass tray in her withered hands, which contained a shrunken head, smothered in a yellow liquid intestinal puss and a cocktail glass of blood with bat venom. She was dressed in a PPE outfit, as all staff members wore, to avoid catching the 'infection'. She gazed around at the pathetic bed-ridden figures. No reply or response, let alone the slightest trace of interest. As the figure turned to leave, one of the patients, a werewolf, strapped to his bed, for his own safety, roared out aloud; his eyes turned from their normal yellow to bright red; a Stage 2 symptom of the fatal dreaded disease.

"Oh, Henreeh! I know you're in a lot of pain. Your once-yellow eyes have now turned red. Soon, it will be time to shift you downstairs. Let me have a word with Dr Psychonster. Err…would you care for a slice of shrunken head?"

"Rrrr!" roared Henreeh, wriggling to be let free.

"Maybe later then, hmm? Alright then, I'll be back again, in a while. Oh, and do remember everyone, to use your pain-ringers, *should the need arise;* thank you all." She turned out the light as it had just turned 9.00 pm, then left.

No sooner had she left, that one of the patients, Mrs Gorelle, a hideous, but cultured ogre on the bed directly opposite to Henreeh, called out eloquently, "We'll all be sorry to see you go, Henreeh. You'll be sorely missed, for sure."

Over the years, she had regarded him as her pet.

Henreeh's contorted face changed to a calm one and he responded with a look on his face which only Mrs Gorelle recognised.

Just then, there was a loud creaking sound; one that was very familiar which all the patients were accustomed to hearing time and time again: the opening of the Hospice's main entrance door, announcing the arrival of new patients. And from the manic cackling laughter, they sounded like Hell's Clowns.

From all the monsters in the Lighthouse Hospice, there were more Hell's Clowns than any other. The reason for this was yet unclear, but one of the theories was that there was some kind of uncanny and genetic link with humans; but this was just a generalised view, still held by the medical team and patients alike. In fact, only *one* had managed to hold onto precious death for two years instead of one, much to the surprise of the nursing team, until the 'infection' took its toll and 'Lucky' as he was nicknamed, dissolved into a red liquid goo which evaporated into, quite frankly, nothingness. And this was the typical manner in which all monsters in hell were dying from the 'infection'.

The pandemic had 'killed off' zillions of monsters as the medical team put their heads together in a desperate bid to develop a vaccine to save them.

Meanwhile, in one of the private medical rooms, a consultant mummy paced up and down the room with one of his witch assistants, holding a pipette in both hands, nervously, facing a beaker on the laboratory desk.

"Alright, Cursella, now very carefully drop some of the serum into the beaker. We don't want any more accidents, do we?" He said, with a look of contempt in his fiery green eyes.

"Of course not, Dr Tep. I...I'm sorry about the incident earlier today."

With the greatest of care, she poured some of the serum, but unfortunately, it smashed in her withered but powerful grip.

"Curses!" cried Dr Tep, infuriated, and extended his right bandaged arm out, towards the door. "Get out, now!"

"I...I'm sorry, Dr Tep; really I am. You...you're making me nervous."

"Leave! Or else I shall have to call the Orc Security Guards to throw you into the river of blood."

As Cursella left, slamming the door, the doctor shrugged and placed his decayed hands over his bandaged face.

"Holy Isis, the kind of monsters I have to put up with! I shall *have* to complain to Satan about her, for sure."

Outside, as if in response, the thunder roared angrily and hailstones began belting down from the dark eerie skies, where gargoyles were in flight, high above the eerie-looking lighthouse.

Suddenly, there was a loud thud, like a falling sound, followed by concerned voices. It was coming from two flights of stairs above one of the wards. At that very moment, Wendella was mid-way up the stairs, sobbing, then went rushing to the room, just in time to see a yellow goo dripping from the bed onto the floor. Unfortunately, one of the patients, known as Alfred-B, had just disintegrated then dissolved into nothingness. Even the goo disappeared swiftly, as was normally the case, so there was never any need to clear up. Cursella looked around wide-eyed at the in-patients; all of which were Hells Skeletons and asked, "Did any of you actually see what happened to Alf before he disintegrated?"

"I did," called out the in-patient directly facing him, from the opposite bed.

"Just before 'the last moment', he called out, almost in a human voice."

"What did he say?"

"He cried out, 'help!' then began to change; liquidate into yellow puss…and…"

"Go on," queried Cursella.

"You'll say I'm out of my mind, but I saw the glimpse of a human face, in a flash, just before it happened."

Cursella sighed, then looked around.

"I…I'm so sorry you all had to witness this. Now, try and rest your tired bones." She turned out the lights, then left.

The following morning, Dr Tep entered the same ward with a medical briefcase. His dishevelled face cracked into a smile, causing some of the decay on his mummified face to fall through the bandages and onto the floor.

"Good news to share, dear in-patients. I think we may have an antidote for the 'infection'. But first, a little briefing. We think we may know where it may have been derived from." He looked around at the skeletons who were seated up attentively on their beds.

"Gargoyles!" He said, in a triumphant tone. "Yes, because only *they* are the ones who have not been affected. We believe that they are spreading it everywhere."

"But gargoyles have been flying around for centuries in hell. Why now?"

Dr Tep shrugged.

"Like us, they too have their own biological anatomy. It's quite possible that it just may possibly have derived from them," he repeated, emphasising.

"That's silly," called out Darkelisa-Z, one of the female skeletons. Each of the skeletons had an alphabetical number tag against their names, to identify them.

"How can you possibly deduce this?"

"Look around you. Each and every monster on our planet is infected; *except* the gargoyles."

"I wonder what Beelzebub has to say about that," retorted Michaellus-R, folding his arms in his bed.

"In any case, I have developed an antidote and need to try it out on a few volunteers." He looked around. "Who would like to go first?"

Once again, there was a loud noise, but this time, it was no thud. It was a pained scream that grew subdued in a few seconds, then a short silence and hissing. Dr Tep's eyes widened in terror and he dropped the large syringe in his left hand, causing the serum to sizzle and dissolve on the floor. He left the ward abruptly and went down to his room, got out a shielding PPE mirror helmet, then continued to basement to the Medusa Ward.

Once there, he kicked down the door, with his mummified right leg and stormed inside. There before him, on the floor, immersed in a pool of blood sat the three daughters of Echidna and Typhon, namely, Stheno, Euryale and the hideous ugly Medusa, with her head of snakes; her head soaked in red blood.

"What do you want in here? Hsss!" called out a threatening monotonous voice from behind the door, that had struck him. Dr Tep moved back and saw a fourth gorgon. This one was male and he was their guardian. His name was Nanas, the guard of Zeus. They were among the oldest in-patients of

Beelzebub's Lighthouse Hospice and the most scary and deadliest. No monster came near them, or turned to stone.

"I heard a loud pained cry. What happened in here?"

"We're having our lunch!" cried Stheno, in a shrilled voice.

"You've committed a murder. I will report you to Dr Psychonster!"

"It is merely a gargoyle that smashed through our ward window. Look." She pointed to a smashed window on the far end of the room.

Dr Tep, raised an eyebrow.

"I have to warn you that in my research, I have found that the 'infection' may derive from gargoyles. But I have devised a serum and would like to try it on all of you; to save your miserable undead lives of course. Now, if you refuse…then you will 'die' a horrible death. The flesh of that wretched gargoyle may just be infected."

They looked at one another helplessly, hissing. Then broke into a fight. Dr Tep gave a sadistic laugh, then left. He locked the door on the way out and made his way back to his private room. At the same moment, outside, the Grim Reaper was bringing in his latest patient; a hideous scarred demon. The hospice doors creaked open and the reaper pointed a bony finger, ushering him to make his way up the stairs. Then, he glided out, slamming the door shut. The demon made his way upstairs and some of the staff, all ogres, appeared and aided him up.

"Oh, we don't often get demons in here. What's your name?"

He stared back at her and replied in a slow, pained voice, due to a slash on his neck.

"Jack."

She engraved his name on a brass armband and placed it around his left arm.

Suddenly, the ground beneath their feet began to shake and Beelzebub's voice echoed around the cold walls.

"Stop! This monstrosity is so evil and capable of unnamed horrors, that he does not deserve *any* form of care in our hospice, let alone a place in HELL. There is only one punishment for him: he will be exiled to earth and be remembered for his evil deeds, as the most infamous killer of all…Jack the Ripper! More so, his real identity will remain unknown forever!"

In a few seconds, 'Jack' vanished and was gone…

The End.

Libitina, Goddess of Funerals and Burials

In the dead of night, in the corner of a desolate space, in pin-drop silence, a cloaked figure with a scythe sat crouched, clenching a dice in her hands; but the 'numerals' etched on it were symbols, representing her victim's fate.

The Grim Reaper reached out her bony left hand, then tossed it to the ground and looked across and gazed at her victim, sneering at his helplessness.

The victim, a young man in his twenties, sat petrified and frozen, awaiting his fate; the sweat pouring profusely down his forehead.

The dice span magically, in slow motion on the wet ground, turning blood-red, ultimately revealing his fate; to be punished in a blaze of flames, but that would only be the finale: after each of his limbs were twisted off very slowly, ensuring he lived and endured all essence of the pain she inflicted, because for him, death was the merciful release of his punishment for Dicing with LIBITINA, Goddess of Funerals and Burials…

That Old Derelict High School

Even after all these years, the Old Derelict High School, which gave Nancy the creeps as a child every time she passed by was still standing, as if announcing its presence. Strangely enough, it had seemed ancient even then.

She would shudder when friends dared her to run her fingers along its large cold stone bricks, which had moss grown over them. She remembered on several occasions, seeing other children playing 'I dare you' and climbing down right onto the ground which was many feet below. In her deepest darkest nightmares, she was convinced that whatever was down there was the essence of pure evil, from night to dawn. In reality, nothing about it ever seemed to change.

"You're not anaemic are you, Mike?" She asked as she served their meal.

"Stop avoiding the question," he replied, placing his arms around her.

Nancy freed herself and retreated back, feeling nervous and irritable. "Okay! If you must know, then *no*, I definitely don't want you going down there again."

Mike sighed and sat at the kitchen table. He loved Nancy and was concerned about her obsession with the Old Derelict High School. She would not talk about it openly. It was as if she was keeping some dark secret about what was there down below, or worse, inside its premises. Its shuttered rooms and windows added to the menace and intimidating factor. She had told him once how she saw a light on, seemingly from out of one of those shuttered windows, and distant moaning sounds. That aroused his curiosity. And so, one night, recently, when he was awoken by Nancy's loud screaming, that was the turning point. He had made up his mind to find out who—or—what—was there.

"I've already made up my mind, Nancy. I'm leaving first thing in the morning."

"No, Mike, I don't want you to go, please stay," said Nancy, placing her arms tightly around him.

"Please don't worry about me. I'll be fine. It's not as if I'm going halfway around the world. It's Scotland, for goodness' sake."

Nancy fell back on the chair with a lost look on her face. She began to fumble and fidget, a sign of nervousness when things were not going the way she would like.

Mike stared at her, then knelt down on the floor beside her. He held her hands and said, "Look at it from this point of view. If I *don't* go, then your health will continue to get worse, mentally and physically, just thinking about that place. And to be frank, I've tolerated enough of your recurring delusions. Besides, you've now aroused my curiosity, so please, dear, just agree and let me go."

He stroked her hands. She looked at him eye to eye, then nodded.

"Good girl. Now, I'm going to get some rest as I need to be up early in the morning. Goodnight." He kissed her and left for the bedroom.

The following morning, Nancy awoke to find her side of the bed empty. She had come up a short while after Mike who was in deep sleep, so she wondered how and when he had left. As she stood up to make the bed, she moved the pillows to one side and saw a note lying on Mike's side. She read it aloud.

Dear, Nancy,

Please forgive me for not staying back, but there's something I did not mention to you. I already went there once before without you knowing. At the time, I was actually climbing down the old school's brick wall and as I jumped to land, I felt something, felt someone or something grab my left leg and bite into my ankle. I fell and was unconscious. When I awoke, I felt a piercing pain on the right side of my neck too. There was fresh blood. Now I HAVE to go back and understand what happened. Wish me well.

With Love,

Mike.

Nancy scrunched up the note and flung it on the carpet, furious and in tears. "He betrayed my trust. All this time, he was lying to me."

Her eyes widened as she realised that tonight, for the first time in her life, she would be alone.

"Oh no-o-o-o!"

Upon reaching Scotland, by train, it was late afternoon as Mike emerged from out the station and boarded the first available cab. "I'd like you to take me to the nearest B&B, please."

Along the way, Mike opened the window and inhaled. "Aah! It feels great to be back in Dundee once again. The air is so fresh and invigorating."

The cabdriver did not say anything, just continued on the route. Mike could only see his eyes through the front seat mirror. He pulled out his tablet from his hand luggage and began to browse.

'I wonder if that Old Derelict High School is still there.' He thought. His fingers had just typed the first few letters then he changed his mind and smiled. *There is no need to anymore. I'll be there in a matter of hours anyway.*

The cab began to slow. At this point, they were passing alongside a massive graveyard.

"Why are you slowing down?" Mike asked, his eyes still on the tablet.

Again, there was no response, but the moment he raised his head up and looked at the glass in front, he noticed that the driver's eyes had turned a scarlet red and from his mouth, live worms were emerging.

"Ahhh!"

Mike reached for the main door button, but it was wedged shut. The cab driver had turned into a zombie and spun around, staring straight at him. He reached forwards and grabbed Mike by his neck, then took a long deep bite.

"Aaaaaahhh!"

Mike found himself lying curled up in the back of the car. His eyes opened and he panicked. He saw the driver staring at him, looking concerned.

"Are you feeling alright, Sir? Just to let you know, we've arrived at the nearest B&B."

Mike sat up and placed his hands over his face and pressed them, ensuring he was wide-awake and in his senses.

"I...I'm so sorry. I think I must have drifted off into sleep."

"You must have been having a nightmare. Your scream alerted me."

Mike got out the car and paid the taxicab driver, then made his way to the bed and breakfast.

'*Alchemists and Ghouls Anonymous.*' He shrugged. "Doesn't sound very inviting, but I need a place to spend a couple of nights at least, so I really have no choice."

After he made his way in, he headed to reception desk where a young lady dressed in jeans and jumper greeted him.

"Good evening, Sir. How may I help you?"

"I'd like to book a room, please, for three nights."

As the girl entered Mike's details in her register, he asked, "Excuse me, but how did you choose such a name for your place?"

"What, you mean, *The Floral Inn Bed and Breakfast*?"

Mike's eyes bulged and he rushed out to see it again. "Oh no, what's happening..."

Moments later, he ran back inside and stared at the receptionist, wide-eyed. His heart beat fast and he was out of breath.

"Are you alright?"

"Y...yes, why do you ask?"

"You're looking very pale. Well, here's the key to your room. Number 666. The boy will show you up."

Mike felt a prod on the back of his legs. When he turned, he saw a small lad standing with a mask over his face. As he made his way up to the room, Mike followed.

At their London flat, it was getting late and Nancy was starting to tremble. She decided to make a cup of tea to help settle her nerves. '*Mike must have reached there by now. I wonder if I should give him a call.*'

She got her mobile phone from her purse and dialled.

"Hello, Mike, how…" Her words stopped as the line was cut.

At the same time, the doorbell sounded. She turned off the kettle and made her way into the hall to open it. Before she did, she stared through the eyepiece on the door.

"There's no one there." She turned away and the doorbell rang again.

"Oh, just a moment." She straightened her dress, opened the door and screamed.

A tall crouched figure entered. Dressed in a long dark suit, he looked like a ghoul, with large penetrating eyes. In a pained and menacing voice, he said. "If you love your husband and want to save his life, then I've come to warn you. Tell him to go back home, *immediately*. I don't want him coming to my Old Derelict High School."

"W…who, or what on earth are you? Are you even human?"

"Do you remember the light at the window there? Your husband may have mentioned it. Well, I am one of the alchemists working at the school. That's *my* room window. No trespassers are allowed in there."

He paused and in the deathly silence, Nancy could hear his loud breathing. Saliva trickled down the left side of his mouth. Then, he raised his hands and began to tear out parts of his face, laughing.

"Oh, well look at the clock. It's 12.00 midnight, the Witching Hour. Ha ha ha ha ha ha ha ha!"

Nancy let out another scream. Seconds later, the alchemist-ghoul vanished. He had come only to convey a warning. Nancy pulled at her hair, agitated and distressed. "I…can't even tell anyone. They'll think I am…"

Tears ran down her face and she stared at the floor and around her. The floor looked spotless and the furniture was where it had always been. Even the bits of the ghoul's flesh and the blood stains had faded away.

"What happens if he comes back again?" She ran for the light switch and turned it on.

Nancy went into the main room and put the TV on. She selected the news channel. At first, the weatherman was reading the forecast around Britain. She sank back on her chair and her eyes began to close.

"Oh, Mike, I miss you so much. I wish you were here with me."

Just then, the scene changed and a video began to play on TV. It featured an old creepy building which looked familiar. It took a moment for Nancy to recognise it, but when she did, her eyes went wide as soup plates.

"That's the Old Derelict High School!"

In the next instant, the same alchemist-ghoul appeared and he stared at her. His long arm reached out from out of the TV set.

"Call him back-NOW!"

"Nooooo!"

*****

Back at the Floral Inn Bed and Breakfast, Mike sat in his room, and unpacked his hand baggage. The window on the front side offered a view of the long winding road which had brought him here.

"Tomorrow, first thing in the morning, I'm heading off to that Old Derelict High School." He stood up and explored the bathroom. He found a shaving kit and an extendable mirror with magnification. The WC had a sealed paper strap across it. Newly washed and folded towels rested on a shower shelf, along with cosmetics in plastic packets.

"Ah, that's really nice. I know I'm going to enjoy it here," he said to himself. "I…" His words were cut short when he noticed something across his neck.

A close-up view in the magnified mirror showed a long deep cut across his throat, which was healing. For a few seconds, he wondered how it got there. Then he recollected his nightmare.

"Oh, my God! It…it means…it *wasn't* a nightmare. I…I really was attacked and bitten by a zombie! It…it means…I'm going to turn into one of those things."

Mike gazed at his hands. His fingernails were turning pale and starting to chip. His teeth had gone yellow and worse, his complexion had turned white as snow.

"I have to get to that Old Derelict High School. I admit at first, it was out of sheer curiosity, but now I have a good reason. I've got to find a cure to my disease."

He wished he could go this moment, but it was too late and he preferred to go in the daylight. Mike stared out the window again. The sky was pitch black; only the full moon was glowing. Something clicked on his door. Mike rushed to open it, but it was locked from the outside.

"What is going on here? I'm going to complain to reception about this."

He went to the phone but he couldn't hear a dial tone. Then an eerie, almost choked and pained voice, sounding from beyond the grave, spoke menacingly:

"Don't dare to come to the Old Derelict High School. If you do, it is your death warrant, and there will be no turning back…hhssss." Then the phone went dead.

"Hello, reception, Angie speaking. How may I help you?" Mike's eyes widened and he broke into a sweat.

"Oh, no, Oh, *no!*"

"Is everything alright, Sir?"

"No, it isn't. Someone has locked my door from the outside. Please help open it."

In a few moments, the door opened and the receptionist came inside, accompanied by the same masked boy.

"Is there anything else I can do for you, Sir?"

"Yes, I wish to lodge a complaint. My door was locked from the outside."

The receptionist ushered the boy who nodded and proceeded to the door lock. In a few moments, he removed a piece of metal that was wedged in the tumbler.

"There you are, Sir. That's what must have wedged it shut."

Mike scratched his head and wanted to say something, but she seemed to be telling the truth.

"Is there anything else I can do for…?"

Upon seeing Mike's repulsive and uncanny features, the receptionist staggered back momentarily, wide-eyed, ushering the boy protectively to one side, then regained her composure.

"I...I'm sorry. I'm just feeling tired. I think I ought to rest."

The receptionist smiled nervously and started towards the door, accompanied by the masked boy. As the door closed, the boy momentarily turned and gazed at Mike who noticed a mischievous look in his eyes.

"Wait, I don' mean to pry, but does he *always* wear that mask?"

The receptionist stopped and replied, "It was a gift from his godmother and he's grown quite attached to it." The masked boy looked at him, smiled eerily and they both left the room.

Mike shrugged. *'Oh well.'*

*****

The next morning, Mike was up early and was out the Inn by 8.30 am. He had ordered a cab to drop him outside the Old Derelict High School. This time, he was taking no chances. He made sure the driver was just as human as he was. They chatted along the way.

"So, where are you from, Sir? If you don't mind me asking."

"London. I was actually here in Glasgow only months ago. I enjoyed it very much, so I decided to come again and, well, here I am!" The driver smiled.

"What's your name?" Mike asked,

"Timothy."

"Nice name. And what else do you do in your spare time, when you're not driving?"

"I study in the late evenings."

"That's nice to know. I believe that education is an integral part of everyone's lives."

"Very true, Sir."

A very long silence followed.

"So, what subject do you study, and where?"

"I study Human Anatomy at the Old Derelict High School."

"Aahhhhhhhhhh!"

The cab skidded, spun, then hit a tree. The cab driver had become engrossed in his talks and lost concentration. The impact of the crash had left Mike with a nasty bump on his head whereas the driver had taken the full blow and lay sprawled across the seat unconscious.

Mike opened his side of the door and staggered out. His body crumpled to the ground and he lost consciousness too.

When he awoke, he found himself right on the outskirts of the Old Derelict High School. It stood there, towering over him. It was exactly 6.00 pm. Mike wished he had a mirror on him to see exactly what he looked like.

As he breathed, he produced a croaking inhuman sound instead of his normal one. Also, he found he had to drag his body forwards. All he could see were his hands. They looked hideous, with protruding green veins. Some had ripped out from his flesh. His mouth trickled with saliva and blood. But now, his priorities had changed, he was determined to survive.

He had no choice but to go down there into the bottom of that Old Derelict High School, just as he did last year. There was one big advantage in his favour; it was daylight.

"Oh, well, here I go." Mike carefully climbed over the rusted poles that made up the outer fencing and once he was on the other side, he glanced down momentarily.

"Oh, gosh. I'd forgotten how far down it is. It's really really deep, like a pit. If I fall, I'll be dead in an instant. I just have to take it nice and slow."

And so, step by step, like a mountaineer, he began to climb downwards. He had come prepared this time and wore his hiking boots which helped him find his footing in the gaps between each of the large stone bricks. Time to time, he kept peering up and down to see how far he had gone.

Within thirty minutes, he could just make out the ground of the school premises.

"Yes! Nearly there now."

Loud clanging sounded from up above. He looked up and spotted a very large object falling in his direction.

"Oh no!"

Without thinking, he jumped.

"Aaah!" It was a clumsy landing and his body curled and twisted into an embryonic posture just as the large object crashed inches away from him.

It was a large wooden crate which resembled a coffin. Surprisingly, it remained intact. He staggered to his feet and retreated as the lid of the crate slowly opened. Mike darted a glance behind him and scrambled for the nearest corner, out of sight. It was starting to get dark, and the porch light was very poor.

He turned the rusty and corroded door knob of the first door he found, but it was locked.

"Oh, no, what am I going to do now?" He said to himself. His voice sounded really terrible. Even he could not recognise it. And then, he remembered the porch window. The window with the light. Maybe if he could identify it and get in, one of the alchemists there could help. Maybe they could cure his infection. Now, in the advanced stages of his metamorphosis, he found it hard to coordinate his movements and in one giant leap, hopped forwards. His body weight had increased as well and he found himself having to drag his weight along as he moved forwards spewing a green odorous slimy drool from his mouth along the way. His boots had split and long green talons protruded trough the leather. And then…

"Stop!" called out a voice. Mike was so petrified, he kept moving as much as he could, to escape whatever it was that had emerged from the crate. But his pursuer caught up with him and a cold, rough hand seized his shoulder. He felt himself being turned around, forcefully, to face whoever was there.

Mike opened his eyes and saw a zombie in a school uniform. Before he could say anything, the zombie clutched his right wrist and began to drag him into the building.

"W…ho who or what kind of monster are you? And where are you taking me?"

The zombie, whose face was a mask of horror, with gashes and bruises, gave a manic laugh. He drooled blood and saliva, some of which dripped onto Mike's clothing. Before long, they arrived at another door. It looked like the main entrance of the Old Derelict High School. He banged at the door and stood with Mike, waiting. Moments later, heavy footsteps could be heard. Something clicked and the door creaked open. A ghoul stood at the entrance and gave a nasty look at the zombie, who let go of Mike and backed away. And then, the ghoul took a bow, gave a sinister smile and said, in a hissing voice:

"Ah, finally you have come. We have been expecting you, **Ghoul Headmaster**; please follow me to your room." And at the same time, there was a distant sound of a light switch as it came on from that same window. But it was too late to find help now.

Mike's eyes widened as understanding dawned. He had changed into a monster just like them. And not just another one, but the biggest monster of them all and now he was a permanent monster of that Old Derelict High School from which there would never ever be any escape; not for him, or any of its staff and pupils, all of whom were monsters of the night.

"Nooooo!"

The End.

Rest in 'Pieces'

He stared down at the deep hole, wiping his forehead and could hear his heartbeat, thumping rapidly, hardly surprising, after two hours of digging strenuously. He gazed down one more time, with a satisfied and content look, then noticed the full moon rising and with a worried look on his face, tossed his victim's remains quickly inside, then felt his pulse race, as the werewolf inside began to awaken and leapt into the hole, in a frenzy, to feast upon the gory human remains…

Cinema Screaming

By the time Oliver Bradley and his partner Cheryl Resole, both in their mid-forties, arrived at the *Blood and Gore Theatre*, for the late-night chiller, the end credits of the previous Greek feature-chiller, *Feast of the Laestrygonians,* were drawing to a close and *Cinema Screaming* began without any intermission. As they made their way inside to locate their seats, they noticed that the entire cinema hall was empty. The glow of the movie reflected on the vacant blue seats which were randomly coated with a thick layer of bright red 'drooling blood', designed to scare the audience.

"Spine-tingling!" remarked Oliver. He then spotted two seats at the centre of the front row. He linked his arms around Cheryl's and they made their way to the seats. As she sat down, she stiffened.

"Are you feeling all right?" He asked.

Cheryl nodded. "I just don't like sitting there. I mean we usually sit in the back row. Here, everyone will be staring at us from behind and we won't even be able to hold hands."

"Good heavens, what do you mean, *everyone?* I mean there's not a single person here. Not even the torch man who was supposed to escort us to our seats." They both glanced back to catch a glimpse of a lean figure, crouching down and making his way along the back row. He sat directly behind them.

"Besides," quipped Oliver. "I'm sure you wouldn't want to sit next to *him* now, would you?"

She smiled and nudged him in the ribs.

"No, of course not."

"And remember, they didn't just name it the *Blood and Gore Theatre* for any reason. Now, let's get our seats, dear; the movie's already started."

Cheryl looked back once more, at the strange figure in the back row. In the dim light, she could just make out his outline as he sat in a fixed pose, eyes bearing down on her.

Oliver took Cheryl's hand, and they proceeded to their seats. They sat and looked up at the screen. The setting was a massive graveyard, in the dead of night, where a young lady was walking barefoot amidst the gravestones, stopping at each one and reading out the epitaphs.

"Where my body rests, so shall it lay until I choose when to awaken…? How weird is that!"

"Angie, come back inside the car. You'll catch your death a cold out there!"

"Yes, in a minute, Finn."

Just then, the night sky lit up as the full moon began to rise.

DS

"Angie. Aaarrgg…"

Finn, who sat in the car, held his throat. His eyes had turned yellow.

"Looks like the old boy's growing stripes! He's changing into a weretiger!" called out Oliver to Cheryl, pointing to the screen.

"Ssh!" She poked him in his ribs with her left elbow. "Don't spoil it, even if you know."

"Ouch! All right, now, what would you like-a Coke, and popcorn, ice cream or maybe salted peanuts?"

"Mmmm, I would fancy some vanilla ice cream, thanks very much."

"All right, I'm going downstairs to get some. I won't be long. You just sit back, relax, and enjoy the movie."

Oliver scurried off to the exit and made his way down a long flight of stairs. As he took the turn at the bottom, the lights went out, so he had to feel his way around the main cinema hallway to the concession stand.

"Hello, is anybody available?" He called out. "I'd like to buy a bag of popcorn please; oh, and some vanilla ice cream too." Oliver waited for what seemed like half an hour, then decided to help himself. He saw a refrigerator with various flavours and sizes of ice cream and other treats, then a packet of popcorn. He placed his selections to one side, then dug into his coat pocket for his wallet. After putting some change on the front counter, he then made his way back through the hall with his purchases and headed upstairs. As he turned toward the stairs, he could hear heavy breathing and clumsy footsteps from behind. He stopped and looked back in time to see a large shadow, which immediately retreated out of sight.

"I'm going to report you when the movie's over!" He shouted.

Oliver then continued back into the cinema room. He could see the back of Cheryl's head.

Cheryl sat slumped in her seat as she watched the movie. In the film, Angie was running through the graveyard, being chased by a weretiger and then a zombie appeared a few yards ahead, with his hands raised in the air, staring at her. Angie's face turned towards Cheryl, her heart beating faster and faster. She appeared to look directly at her, pleading,

"Oh, please help me, Cheryl. I...I don't want to die. Please help me, quickly!" To Cheryl's surprise, Angie reached out her arm through the screen towards her.

"No! This can't be happening! It...IT'S JUST IMPOSSIBLE." Cheryl trembled, taken aback and startled. Seconds later, she felt a hand over her shoulder, and she screamed.

"Hey, relax! It's only me, Oliver, your date for tonight, remember?"

Cheryl was perspiring and gasping for breath. She reached into her handbag for her inhaler and took two puffs. Oliver sat beside her, still clinging onto the popcorn and ice cream, which he placed on his lap. He held both of her hands gently.

"Listen, I'm sorry. If I had known you were going to get so jumpy, I would have never left you alone."

Cheryl turned to him, gazing wide-eyed, then replied in a broken and shaky voice. "Oliver, did you see what just happened?" Her voice trembled.

"No, I was busy looking at you. Here, you better eat you ice cream before it melts."

"This can' be real." Cheryl nodded vehemently to herself. "Damn it, Oliver, just listen to me! That girl in the graveyard,

Angie, looked right at me, then reached out through the screen and cried for help."

Oliver pursed his lips and looked at the screen, then back at Cheryl, caressing her blonde hair. "Come on. We're both grown-up adults. I mean, *listen* to how you sound. You must have a vivid imagination; I'll grant you that. Besides, it's not uncommon for any of the characters to gaze at the audience, particularly at live theatre stage shows. It's called 'soliloquy,' especially in Shakespearian plays."

"Then *how do you explain* her hand coming out the screen and reaching for me?"

Trying hard to keep a straight face, Oliver diverted his eyes once again to the movie. Angie was still caught up between the weretiger and the zombie. She lost her balance and sprawled on the grass. Just then, the weretiger's eyes attention turned toward the zombie. It pounced on him, biting into his neck and tearing through its jugular veins, then ripped off its head and tore it to shreds.

"Eeuuww, now that is gruesome!" Oliver tore open his bag of popcorn and offered it to Cheryl. She refused, and he popped some in his mouth. As he bit down, he felt something soft, like jelly, swimming inside. It felt repulsive and he spat it out.

"Oh, that's sickening!" It was a yellow eyeball.

"Gggrrrr!" roared the weretiger in the movie and gazed straight into Oliver's eyes, like a predator stalking his prey. To his shock, it only had one eye. Then, it began creeping towards him menacingly, on its hind legs, until it covered the entire screen and looked down at Oliver who sat quivering on his seat. Oliver's jaw fell; his hands grew sweaty and slack, causing his popcorn to spill on the floor. He turned toward

Cheryl who was placing her inhaler back into her handbag. She gave no sign of noticing. He was about to cover his eyes but dared to look back at the screen and the logo INTERMISSION appeared. The curtains fell, but it was still dark. He heaved a sigh of relief and then noticed that the ice cream on her lap was melting.

"Cheryl! Look, your dress!"

She looked down at the stain.

"Oh no, that's my new frock. I wore it especially for tonight." She set the ice cream on the floor and stood up, wiping the stain with a tissue from her handbag. But then, she felt something cold and wet running down the back of her neck. She shuddered and reached behind, but afraid to touch. She turned to Oliver.

"Would you mind taking a look?"

He stood up and examined the back of her dress. Then, his eyes bulged.

"Oh, my God! Y…you must be hurt. Your dress is torn and soaked with blood, and it's still oozing. Quick, let's go to the restroom now, and please don't argue." He grabbed her right hand and they proceeded downstairs to the exit, but again, when he turned, a large misshapen shadow was looming on the wall, breathing heavily. This time, Oliver could tell that the shadow belonged to something inhuman.

"We need to turn back, or confront it." Oliver took Cheryl back into the cinema hall to their seat and carefully peeled the ripped dress from her back to have a closer look.

"Oh no; no it can't be."

"Can't be what?" Cheryl asked, curious and agitated.

"Cheryl, don't ask me how, but there's a claw mark on your back."

No sooner had his words come out when the claw mark faded. Seconds later, her back completely healed.

"Am I dreaming, or am I going insane?"

He retreated. "It's gone now. How are you feeling?"

"Perfectly all right. But I'm now worried about you, Oliver."

He took off his coat and placed it around her, to cover her bloodstained and torn dress.

"Don't worry about the dress. I'll buy you a new one." He caressed her cheeks and then his expression changed to concern.

"Listen, Cheryl, I know this is going to sound absurd. Maybe you'll even think me insane, but you've got to listen to what I have to say."

She turned towards him attentively. "All right, I'm all ears."

"Just before the intermission, something strange happened and I did not imagine it. My popcorn had that weretiger's eye in it and now he wants it back. There, I said it." He waited for Cheryl's reaction. There was a moment's silence, after which she burst into a fit of frenzied laughter.

"Well, after intermission, when that red curtain rises, we'll both find out, won't we?" She folded her arms.

"Yes but…"

"I don't care what you say anymore, so there! Now you got a taste of your own medicine, and you expect me to believe every single word you said. I mean, can you see how it must feel now, to have someone doubt you when they're telling the truth?"

"Okay, I admit, I was wrong." For a moment, they both grew quiet, as if reminiscing on their experiences, after which Oliver's eyes brightened. He snapped his fingers.

"Of course. How silly of us. Maybe it's all a setup; you know, as part of a gruesome cinematic experience to thrill and chill audiences."

"More like frighten the daylight of the audiences! Huh, no wonder, there's not a single person here except that weirdo in the back row."

Cheryl turned around to glance. He was lying on his seat with his throat slashed.

"Oliver, *look!*" He turned around.

"Oh, my God!" Oliver stood up and held her right arm. "Let's go and take a look. No, on second thoughts, it's best you wait here. It's a severed body, and I don't want you having nightmares."

As Oliver made his way upstairs to the top balcony, the curtains began to rise and second half of the movie resumed. Cheryl's attention was split between Oliver and the movie. She sat on the edge of her seat, biting her nails, unaware of the specks of dry red nail paint falling on the floor.

The camera focused on the twilight sky, as the sun began to rise, then fell on the weretiger, who had begun to change into his human form. When he did, Cheryl gasped.

"No! It can't be, Frank, is that *really* you?"

She stood up from her chair, ecstatic. He was her former sweetheart, she recalled.

"Frank, *it is you!*"

But in her excitement, she momentarily forgot that supernatural forces were at large. The movie had developed a mind of its own with its characters interacting with the audience. As Cheryl retreated to her chair, in the movie, there followed a loud frantic scream from behind as Frank turned to see Angie being attacked by the same zombie who had now re-assembled itself.

More corpses were pulling themselves out from the earth and making their way towards her. Now semi-nude and vulnerable, Frank glanced around desperately for a weapon to fight the zombies.

In the back row, Oliver was examining the dead body when he also heard the scream. For the first time, his eyes fell on Angie.

"No, it can't be! It's the spitting image of the girl I was dating." From where he stood, he could see Cheryl a few yards ahead, seated in the front row. Then, as he made his way down the long middle aisle, there was another loud scream as the zombie bit into Angie's left arm, tearing off her hand. She fled from her undead pursuers in the graveyard and straight towards the screen. Cheryl crouched back in her seat; her eyes squeezed shut. In that instant, there followed a loud thud as Angie ran out from the screen and fell to the floor of the theatre.

By now, Oliver had reached the front row in time to see Angie, her left hand decapitated from her arm and blood spurting out, as she made a dash towards Cheryl.

"Cheryl! Run for your life!" he yelled at the top of his voice. "She's become one of the un-dead. Just run, before she bites you!"

Meanwhile, Frank was now watching them through the movie, but the zombies had surrounded him, and he had to make a split-second decision. He bent down and charged straight into one of them, which sent both him and the zombie crashing out of the screen and tumbling onto the cinema floor. Frank looked around for a weapon to fight off the zombie, as Oliver and Cheryl made a run for the exit, closely followed by Angie. The zombie staggered to grab hold of Frank, but he kicked it away with his right leg, and it landed on the front seat where Cheryl had been sitting.

Oliver and Cheryl clutched each other's hand and hid in a recessed wall along the corridor, in a desperate bid to lose Angie.

"Sshh! Not a word," he whispered, sweat perspiring from his hands.

Cheryl, who was asthmatic was wheezing. She reached for her inhaler in her handbag, but as she pulled it out, it toppled onto the floor and rattled out of sight.

Angie, who had reached the corridor, heard the sound. She peered toward the recess and caught sight of them. Her face beamed and she burst out in harsh laughter. She retreated, then bumped into Frank, who had just caught up with her.

"Perfect," he said to her. "They're cornered now, and that's *just* where we want them. Hah, hah, hah, hah, hah!"

They held hands and retreated to the cinema hall, leaving Oliver and Cheryl.

"W-what did they mean, *'just where we want them,'* hmm?" Cheryl gasped, out of breath and nauseous.

Before Oliver could reply, loud thudding footsteps bounded up the stairway. He looked right and left. Angie and Frank at one end and at the stairway, plodding footsteps. They were trapped both ways.

What was making its way up the stairs?

Cheryl's face turned pale. Gasping for air, she fell unconscious, slumping into Oliver's arms.

"Look, whoever you are, please leave us alone," Oliver begged. "We just want to get out of here in one piece."

The footsteps stopped and the shadow froze in the same position it previously had when Oliver first saw it. He could make out a large looming shadow on the wall. A pin-drop silence followed, which seemed to last for eternity. And then, for the first time, the shadow became real. There, in front of him, stood a giant hairy cannibal; a Laestrygonian, which Oliver assumed had made its way out from the previous movie. It held a huge rock in both of its hands, gave a loud roar then rammed it straight onto Oliver's head. The head sheared off his body and spun into the beast's hands. The Laestrygonian devoured it in one gulp, then proceeded to the remains of its victim's body, enjoying the late-night feast.

In the meantime, Frank was changing into a weretiger and Angie, into a full-fledged zombie. Once they had, both proceeded down the stairway to join the Laestrygonian, whom they had named 'Wonderer', in one glorious bloody feast, after which they would return to their respective features and await their next forthcoming victims.

They would re-emerge—but only when the time was right…

The End?

Demon-Priest

Voodoo dolls lay tossed across the blood-soaked floor, where the voodoo priest lay crouched. The impaled spear, impaled straight through his head, protruding from out his skull, with filaments and specks of his brain, still seeping out the corners of the spear, oozing out eerily; but most uncanny of all was the expression on his face, for there was a smile on it: the last sensation he felt, upon sacrificing his Soul to the Demon-Priest…

Tiara, Zombie-Girl

The sun was setting as the ferryboat came to a steady halt against the Caribbean desert island. The ferry man, a tall bearded man who had not spoken a word throughout the journey, suddenly gave a loud knock to the passengers below. A gaunt man in his thirties was the first to emerge from inside, followed by a frail woman in her twenties. They were good friends and had recently been engaged. The soft cool night breeze greeted them as they made their way off it and onto the island filled with palm trees.

"Are we the only ones to arrive here?" She asked, placing her arms around his waist. He turned towards her and gave her a menacing look.

"No, of course not. Banshees, demons, zombies, werewolves and vampires all await us, over there." He pointed ahead, wide-eyed. She suddenly squeezed tightly against him.

"Oh, Richard, please stop. You know I'm faint-hearted and this is supposed to be our summer vacation resort." He looked around as far as he could but there was no one in sight.

"You know, Jill, come to think of it, you may be right." He walked a few paces forwards and continued looking around and then scratched his chin thoughtfully.

"Oh no, Richard! Where's the ferry? I mean, we only just got off it." Richard swiftly turned around to see open space. Only the sea was visible.

"That's odd; where on earth did it go? It's late. Come on, Jill." He said, holding her hand and began walking.

"But where to?" He pointed ahead where a small distant cottage could barely be seen. "I'm sure if there is anyone here, then they must be in there waiting to welcome us."

"Oh really, and what makes you so sure?"

"Because, there's a candle flickering in there."

A short while later, as they arrived at the cottage, suddenly, a young native girl of exotic beauty appeared in front of them dressed traditionally. She had a mop of dark fuzzy hair and wore sparkling green emerald earrings.

Around her neck was a red ruby necklace and around her wrists were matching bangles. Her feet were bare and she wore golden anklets around them. She held a golden tray with some snacks and beverages. But despite her dress-sense, there was definitely something sinister and eerie about her face and hands which were prematurely aged and wrinkled. Most prominent of all were her eyes that appeared to be blank and staring right though them.

Jill froze in her tracks, completely petrified.

"Welcome to Zombie-Island. M...my name...is Tiara. Food...take." She placed the tray rather clumsily on the ground and suddenly vanished into thin air.

"Aaaahh! D...Did you see that, Richard?" Jill cried, hysterically.

"Hmm?" She turned to find him gazing at the gold tray.

"I can't believe this is happening. First, the ferry and now her! Richard, are you listening to me!" Jill grabbed and shook him.

"Oh, for goodness' sake, just listen to yourself. How can you talk such balderdash, hmm? I mean it's getting dark and we've had a really long and tiring trip abroad that ferry."

"Well, whose idea was it to come to Jamaica for a hot summer's vacation?" She asked, accusingly.

"Mine, of course. I'm not denying it." Richard noticed tears pouring down her eyes.

"Hey, don't cry. I hate tears." He reached out his hands to wipe them away, but she pushed him away.

"Don't touch me! You don't know anything about feelings. All you're interested in is that stupid gold tray. I could see that look in your eyes. It's there even now."

"I'm sorry. I didn't mean to…" Suddenly, Jill stormed off into the cottage. He turned back to where the gold tray lay and lifted it off the ground. He then carried it into the cabin and placed it on the table where a bowl of fruits and nuts lay beside a kettle and a dish containing large coffee beans.

"Mmm, this cake smells absolutely delicious, and it's still warm." He carefully cut a slice off with the bread knife nearby.

"Look, I'm really very sorry. I shouldn't have spoken to you like that, but you must eat something first." He handed her an apple and sat beside her with a slice of cake. It had a strange meaty texture to it.

"I wonder who baked it. It couldn't surely be Tiara! You know, I'm going to find out where she stays and where her parents are. I'm also going to find out exactly who else lives on this desert island; there are so many questions on my mind about this place."

He stood up and stretched.

"Look, Jill, it's been a long day for both of us. Let's catch up on some beauty sleep. In the morning, we'll go Witch-Hunting, hah ha ha." Jill did not like this remark and began to sulk.

"Hey, look, I'm sorry. I was just trying to…"

"Scare me!" She retorted. Her face began turning pale and her pupils were dilating, as she suffered from epilepsy.

"No, on the contrary, I was just trying to cheer you up."

"Well, that's not how you go about doing it! Goodnight!" She stormed across to bed with her handbag and took out some pills for her condition and popped them in her mouth. She then lay down on it, turning her face away from Richard and against the wall.

The following morning, Richard awoke to discover Jill was missing. At first, he retained his composure and called out to her. When there was no reply, he got out of bed abruptly and began searching around the hut. In fact, there was only one separate room, the bathroom, and she wasn't there either.

"Jill!" Still no reply. He ran outside and looked around. This time, he shouted out at the top of his voice.

"Jill!" But the only response was the sound of the sea waves crashing against the rocks, rustling tree leaves and the whistling cool breeze that blew on his cheeks. As he moved forwards, the rays of the sun also greeted him. Richard stopped in his tracks. His thought hard where she might have gone. In frustration, he kicked some sand with his feet.

"Curses! Why all the mystery. Why all the suspense?" He continued to talk to himself. "It's my entire fault. I shouldn't have frightened her with all that nonsense about withes and demons. Come to think of it, she was rather upset last night, to say the least."

Just then, Richard heard a loud cry for help followed by crackling sounds. He looked upwards at the palm trees ahead of him and could see large clouds of smoke emerging and the crackling of flames. The cry sounded like it belonged to Jill and so Richard ran as fast as he could, calling out very loudly, "Hold on, I'm on my way!"

He raced forwards in the direction and by the time he reached the flames, he got the shock of his life.

"Oh no! Please, no! Jill!"

There was a huge fire and inside it, engulfed in flames, Tiara and Jill stood, embracing one another. And then, the flames began to change colours every few seconds. It was already too late to save either of them, or was it? He tore off his shirt and raced forwards straight into the flames and placed it around them and then, with all his might, pushed them both out of the flames and onto dry land. He then rolled frantically onto the ground with the two of them still in his grip until all the flames had evaporated. After this, something even more sinister happened. The two of them just vanished.

"What on earth is happening? Where are they? I could swear they were as real as me. I touched them. They were right here beside me. Am…am I going crazy?"

Tired and confused, as he made his way to the cottage, he suddenly stumbled and fell over something hard embedded in the ground. He looked at it and pulled it out. It was a book with illustrations.

"*Zombie-Island*. Hmm, how extraordinary. I'm going to take it with me and read through it. It may contain some important clues about this place."

It was night time and Richard lay on the bed reading through its pages very carefully. The book was full of shocks and surprises. The title, did not take much guessing as it would fully read *Zombie Island* on the inside cover. It was in fact not a book, but a diary written by a visitor to the island over two centuries ago and his name was unanimous. Just the letters **LM,** which were his abbreviations. The first entry, he read out to himself,

Just arrived this evening. Upon arrival at the cottage, a girl called Tiara appeared.
Strange yet hospitable child. Served me food and just vanished into thin air.

"Oh my God! The same as with us!" He flicked through to the end of the week.

Day seven and I'm not feeling comfortable being stranded here alone. I've taken precautions against the zombies by using my lighter to make a fire each night outside the cottage. It's the only place I feel safe. Though I can hear them crowding around the place every night. I know for a fact they want to devour my body. God help me.

Richard slammed the book shut, perspiring. He suddenly felt very insecure.

"I've made a very terrible and extremely stupid mistake that could cost me my life. I shouldn't have removed those bodies from the fire. It must have started off naturally, like those forest fires...and I had to interfere." He looked at the cottage door to see if there was a lock. There wasn't.

"Damn it!" His heart beat very fast and he decided to use the large table to block it as a precaution for his own safety. He then flicked the diary forward to the middle. It was blank, so he turned back a couple of pages to the last few entries and continued to read.

God, I'm feeling so hungry, but there's nothing out there. Even the coconuts are contaminated, and besides, I can't go out anymore. Not safe. Tiara still brings food but has sided with 'them' for some time now and is trying to take bites out of my arm to turn me into one of 'them'.

'*Hmm.*' Thought Richard. "I should be very careful of her, if she turns up." He skipped a couple of pages to the penultimate one and then continued reading.

'*Something's started happening to me. The food Tiara left...*' Richard gasped. "Is that it? Oh well, here goes then, last page."

Suddenly, there was a chilling scream in the distance. He rushed to the cottage window and looked out. A shiver ran down his spine.

It was pitch black outside now and nothing was visible. He couldn't venture out either.

There was no alternative but to ignore it and return to his bed.

"Okay, here goes, last page." Richard lay down and read out aloud.

Too weak to write anymore. Just realised, I made a fatal error. The zombies were using Tiara as their instrument to give me contaminated food to turn me into one of them and I fell into their trap…

The diary dropped from Richard's hands and his face turned pale as he realised now what was happening to him.

"Oh, my God! I had a bit of everything Tiara offered me. It means…it means."

Something else suddenly entered his mind. If Tiara could appear and disappear, then what was preventing her appearing inside the cottage, despite the door being blocked. For the first time, he began to feel very frightened and insecure. He also realised that this was in fact his last stance, against all the odds. And then, as if she had been reading his thoughts, Tiara suddenly appeared before him inside the cottage itself.

"Aaaahh! Y…your face! What happened to your face for God's sake?"

Tiara stood before him, still sizzling from her burns.

"T…the flames. Y…you saved my life. And now, I must serve you for the rest of your life."

"B…but I don't want to be served by you. Y…you're not even human. I read about you in **LM's Diary**."

"You…found the diary? The diary of Leonard Mitchell?" Richard's eyes lit up.

"Did you say Leonard Mitchell? Oh, my God! His was one of the names on my family tree. It means…he was one of my ancestors."

"S…so you must be…Richard Mitchell."

"Yes, that's rather obvious. Look, Tiara, if you're really serious about wanting to help me, then please tell me where my Jill is. I...saved you both from that fire. Where is she?"

Tiara began to shed tears for the first time.

"Oh no. Please don't tell me she's dead."

"She is not...dead. But, she is now one of us. S...she has been tasted, so she changed...just like me."

"What do you mean?" Richard said, alarmed.

"Why... don't you take a look... outside from the window?"

Richard rushed up to the window and staggered at the sight before him. There was a dark figure staring right back at him, eye to eye and yet, her features were not clear. He ran past Tiara and outside.

"Jill, is that you? Thank God, I found..." His words were cut as the figure started walking towards him slowly and eerily, reaching out its arms. Like Tiara, they too were burnt and sizzling, while her face was numb and expressionless. Blood oozed from out her mouth as she opened it wide. And then; she charged right up to him in a split second and took a long deep bite.

"Aaaahh!"

The End?

Frenzic Bite

The un-dead are coming at you, this Halloween. 'Corpses' from every creek and corner you can imagine.

Some are slow, while others are fast, All awakening from their long deep slumber, hungry for flesh, thirsty for blood.

Beware their frenzic bite!

Charaal

The museum was very well maintained considering its age. As a matter of fact, it was estimated to have been built in the sixteenth century. Every so often, 'items' appeared in dark corners or inconspicuous places where no one visited. They were only hit upon when workers came to make changes or do repair jobs. The keeper appeared as ancient as the museum. He held no account of his age, but had long white hair down to his shoulders and a bushy beard and moustache and hairy eyebrows that met in the middle. However, he did maintain a good sense of humour and would often joke that he was a victim of lycanthropy and had been related to the notorious Gilles Garnier.

That fateful Halloween night, John and Sally Redwood's car had run out of petrol during a spell of heavy rain and thunder outside. One would imagine, this was the perfect setting for a thriller. But everyone had their own destiny and the fate that lay ahead for these two love-birds was far more than could be imagined.

The doors of the museum were banged from outside. There was so much rain and speeding winds that it could barely be heard. Nonetheless, the museum keeper made his way slowly to the doors which creaked as he opened them.

"Please, may we come in? Our car's out of petrol and we're lost. We won't stay long, that's a promise. Just allow us to stay until the storm dies down."

"You can both stay as long as you like. It's no skin off my nose," replied the museum keeper. He escorted them to a private room where a cosy wood fire was crackling and excused himself while he prepared some warm food and drink for them.

John turned to Sally with a look of surprise.

"Can you believe it? We're actually spending the night inside a museum!"

"Yes and it's very old by the looks of it, and that keeper, he looks as old as the museum itself."

"What does it matter, John? It's so kind of him to take us in and allow us to spend the night."

"Are you joking? I'm not going to spend the night in this creepy place!"

"Oh, not even with me beside you?" She caressed his hands.

"Well, if you put it that way, then…alright."

"Dinner is served. By the way, I'm *not* a butler," said the museum keeper, trying to maintain his wit. John and Sally stood up and followed him into another room with a beautiful antique table.

"This is a really wonderful table," said John.

"That's what Frederick-II said when he ate his last meal here, before they beheaded him."

"Euugghh!" said Sally.

"So, do you watch a lot of Marx Brothers movies, Mr Museum Keeper?"

"When I have nothing better to do, yes. Now, please be careful what you say or else, I'll throw my dirty handkerchief in your plate." He smirked.

Sally kicked John's legs under the table, ushering him to keep quiet. After all, they were guests here.

"I want to thank you sincerely, from the bottom of my heart," said Sally. "Er, both our hearts I mean."

"Hey, slow down, one beat at a time. Thank you, thank you." He stood up and took a bow.

John helped himself to some tomato soup and scattered bread crumbs inside.

"Mmmm, this is really delicious. Did you prepare it may I ask?"

"No. That was Charaal, my wife." They both turned to one another.

"Well, there's no need to look so surprised. I may be as old as a mummy, but a man needs his share of companionship too."

"Charaal must be quite old I imagine," said Sally. "Is she not joining us for dinner?"

"No, she prefers to stay on her own most of the time. It's just this place. I think it's affected both of us. We've been here for a long time."

John finished his soup and helped himself to a bowl of nuts. Suddenly, he began to chirp and started hopping around on two legs. He saw a wall and climbed up on it.

"Aaaah!" screamed Sally. "W...What's happened to John?"

"I'm sorry, it must be the left-overs the squirrels decided to leave behind. Don't worry, the effect will wear off. In the meantime, come on, I'll show you around the place and if we're lucky, we might catch a glimpse of Charaal." He raised both his eyebrows mischievously. Sally followed him out, still staring at John who was munching nuts on the wall. He tossed one at her.

The museum consisted of very large halls and there were narrow corridors that appeared every few metres that led to another direction. There were benches to sit as well. The animal and human exhibits were moulded in plastic and clay while the older relics were seemingly original fossils and excavations of birds, mammals and reptiles. Suddenly, John appeared from behind.

"Hey, wait for me," Sally gave him a tight hug.

"John, you're alright, thank goodness. You were behaving like a squirrel and munching nuts on the wall."

"Was I?" He scratched his head with his left hand. Sally burst out laughing at his lost expression. Suddenly. the museum keeper was not there.

"Now where did he go?" John quipped.

"Oh my gosh, look!" The museum keeper was crawling on the floor on his stomach, sliding along. John and Sally couldn't resist laughing.

"Hah hah hah hah hah hah hah hah hah!" laughed John.

"Ahh aahh haa haa haa haa haa. Hee hee hee hee hee!" laughed Sally.

"Go on, laugh if you must," replied the museum keeper. "But I must remind you that this museum belongs to me and my wife and I can do as I please."

"But what are you doing?" John cried, hysterically.

"I do snail-paces at this time every night. It helps stimulate and strengthen my digestive tract, if you must know, but don't you try it. It's just something I do that works for me." He stood up and brushed the dust off his clothes.

Suddenly, they heard an oboe playing in the background.

"Charaal!" said the museum keeper and ran forwards and vanished down the corridor.

"Quick, let's follow him," said John and held Sally's right hand. Both ran and caught a glimpse of him just as he shut a door. He could be heard talking to Charaal.

"Alright, this is the big moment. Are you ready, Sally?"

"I'm with you all the way. Here goes, one, two, three!" John turned the handle and barged in with Sally.

"Oh my God! This can't be true!" said John, turning to Sally in deep surprise. There, before them stood the museum keeper and beside him was a giant pink squid in a tank. Oboe music played in the background from two speakers connected to a DVD player.

The museum keeper turned to them and said, in a soft voice,

"Meet, Charaal. Isn't she beautiful?"

"Pleased to meet you, John and Sally. I hope you enjoyed your meal. I made it with my own tentacles."

"Aaahhhh!" They screamed.

The End.

The Gates of Hell

In the deathly silence of that inauspicious, unholy night, the dense mass of heavy fog gradually began to fade away revealing in the distance, a robed bony figure, slightly stooped, accompanied by a large black ominous raven, on a boat.

The manifestation is none other than the Angel of Death! And as he reaches out his scythe, at unwary and unsuspecting souls, ruthlessly severing their spirits from their bodies, claiming them, then returns back promptly to the Gates of Hell.

The Witching Seed

It was Halloween night and as Jill Berry, a young lady in her twenties, was preparing to go to bed, she heard pained sounds coming from her backyard. She tiptoed cautiously to her kitchen and peered through the blinds. To her astonishment and shock, she saw an elderly lady dressed as a witch, lying on the grass, wreathing in pain. Beside her lay her broomstick.

"Please, help me, someone…aaahh!"

Jill opened the door and rushed out instantly to have a closer look and helped her to her feet.

"W…who in blazes are you? And what are you doing in my garden?"

"Sorry, dear, but I was flying on my broomstick and lost my way in the dark then crash-landed here!"

In appearance, she seemed to be in her early seventies, crouched and wore a turfy black pointed witch hat and a dark cloak. On her hands, she wore red mittens and she held a wicker-basket with some Candy Pumpkin and all sorts of things. She lifted her broomstick to inspect it, then smiled once satisfied it was still intact.

"Questions questions. You really must learn to trust, Ms Jill Berry."

"H…how did you know my name?"

"Oh, I know everything about you. Unfortunately, I don't really have a name, but I want to give you back something for your kindness."

The witch reached out one of her withered hands with long black talons.

Jill retreated back a few steps momentarily as she felt a chill run down her spine. She wasn't the kind of person who enjoyed mysteries or pranks of any kind. The lady sensed this and smiled.

"The seed!" retorted the woman.

"I'm sorry?" Jill replied startled and totally lost in confusion.

"Yesterday morning, you threw a seed on the spot where I'm standing."

"You're a liar. Now, get out of my garden and leave my house."

"Alright, then, let me try and tell you my version of the truth. That 'lemon' seed you tossed in the garden last night, Jill, it was no ordinary seed. It was the only one of its kind, known as the Witching Seed; **I am that seed**. I grew overnight after the rainfall and now you can ask me for *any* wish you like."

Jill coughed and thought for a moment.

"Alright, I'll play along, but then you must leave right away, or else I'll call the police. So, tell me, witch, just how many wishes do I have?"

"Two."

"Isn't that meant to be three?"

"Two wishes only."

It took a few moments for Jill to decide and when she had, she could hardly contain herself. The witch sensed this and her face turned hard and pale.

"Ms Berry, I only ask that you be very careful what you wish for."

"Yes, thank you for that, but I've made up my mind. I wish…I wish that all men find me irresistible."

The lady's eyes gleamed and a yellow glow filled her eye balls then vanished.

"It is done."

Suddenly, before Jill could reply, the witch sunk into the ground from where she had sprouted and grown. Jill could not believe her eyes and walked up to the spot and stared down. She then gave a shrug and went indoors and stared in the mirror.

"I still look and feel the same. I knew it. That old witch was just bluffing." She gave a disappointed shrug, turned off the lights and went to bed.

The following morning, the doorbell rang and when Jill went to open the door…

"Oh my word!" There, in front of her was an endless queue of men holding red roses and gifts of all sorts. They all began making their way in one by one. The house was soon completely full of men who were making advances at her and throwing flowers at her in admiration, but after sometime, Jill began to get scared as it wasn't ending. She rushed out to the garden trying to retain her composure but the men all followed her wherever she went. Jill reached the spot where the lucky seed was and closed her eyes, as if willing the witch to re-appear and rescue her.

"Oh, please re-appear. I'm really scared now." Suddenly, the ground stirred and before her eyes, Jill saw the witch rising eerily out the ground.

"Oh, my God! H...how did you. Never mind. I'm just glad you're here. Thank God! Where were you?"

The elderly lady gave a coy smile and replied, "Too many questions, Jill Berry. I know exactly how your mind works and what you're thinking. When you asked for your first wish, I realised right away how foolish you were and that you were going to regret it."

"Th...then why didn't you stop me?"

"I am here only to serve and nothing more."

The men were still around Jill, caressing her and throwing red rose petals at her, from head to foot. Some of them sang lullabies and love songs to praise her beauty. Jill stared hard at the witch.

"This is not my second wish, but could you please make them all go away!" The witch picked up a piece of candy apple from her fruit basket and tossed it at her.

"Take a large bite. It has the power to reverse the spell." And so, Jill took a bite and a few men vanished. Likewise, the more she ate, the more men vanished.

"This is fun!" she said. The elderly lady peered at her and nodded her head slowly from left to right.

"You still have not learnt from your mistake. But I am helpless and have no choice but to ask you your second and final wish."

Jill thought hard and carefully.

"I wish...I wish I could fly like a bat, high up in the sky, gliding over the night skies and to the stars."

Jill noticed the elderly lady's eyes filled with menace and once again, there was a bright glow. This time, the glow was red and then her eyes turned normal.

"It is done. Now, it is time for me to go."

Before Jill could reply, the elderly lady sunk down into the earth once more. Perhaps for the last time. Jill wondered if she would ever see her again. Just as Jill turned to head off inside and check what changes had taken place, she suddenly felt herself lift upwards. It's as if there was no gravity. Higher and higher she rose.

"Whooo! Look at me! I'm just like a bat!" She continued to rise higher and higher until she topped the clouds. She felt a tinge of pain in her throat and suddenly lost her voice and began to scratch and claw after which her arms began to change into web-wings and her feet too. She just kept flapping and flapping and after some time, it was not fun anymore…

It was really cold up in the sky and it was only then that she realised in horror that she was trapped permanently in the body of a vampire bat for the rest of her natural life, and this time, there was no turning back…

The End.

Beware, the Undead

Halloween is *finally here…*

So, beware the Undead Clown; ghosts, spirits and corporal beings, including zombies and vampires, fiends that prey and feast on your flesh and blood, rejoicing in their evil ways.

Sentenced to exist in a permanent state of limbo, these tortured and tormented dark souls seek to resolve their misfortunes by vengeance on the innocent as a means to end their imprisoned and cursed state of being.

Nachzehrer, Lonesome and on the Prowl

High up in the cold and dark night skies, glides the Nachzehrer, in bat form, lonesome and on the prowl.

Always on the lookout for fresh blood, seeking out more innocent victims, this centuries-old, soul-sucking vampire is just *one* of its kind, and also, the deadliest.

A bizarre mix of ghoul and vampire, it promises to 'terrify', and even in its 'human form', is repulsive and gruesome to see.

Pale-skinned, with uncanny features, this un-dead fiend suddenly spots its next victim then glides down instantly, morphing into a tall lean cloaked figure.

It creeps up from behind, stalking its unsuspecting prey, then tightly grabs viciously into his flesh, with its long black talons.

Shocking and petrifying its latest victim, then hypnotises it with his menacing glowing-green eyes, and sinks its venom, through razor-sharp fangs, puncturing through the jugular-vein, relishing and satisfying its monstrous and heinous craving for human bloodlust.

Strigoi: Grand-Daddy of All Vampires

Run away, while you can; save your souls,
For I am the Strigoi; grand-daddy of all vampires!
Risen from my grave, I roam the earth, once more,
Invisible and able to transform into any animal I choose.
Yes, I am indeed a creature of demonic lineage; a vampire menace
To be feared by all! I dig up graves and feast on the dead,
So be warned; I am here to eliminate all beings!
Do I run a shiver down your spine!?
Then hide away wherever you wish;
For I am the Strigoi, and will find you, sooner or later,
Hah hah hah hah hah!

Skyrim, Headless Horseman

Watch out and beware, the next Hessian, better known as Skyrim, Headless Horseman, a phantom who'll send shivers down your spines, as he gallops randomly on his ethereal horse; the next time you decide to venture out; especially along a lonely country trail in autumn time, for that is when you'll see him 'galloping' leaving a smoky blue trail behind it, and harmless as he may seem, be warned, for he carries a sharpened axe behind his back!

Right Time Right Place

A piteous wailing moan echoed the air, as night turned to dawn. Emma stopped momentarily to catch her breath and look around. The path was very steep—a real scramble. Far beneath her, the sea waves crashed about wildly against the jagged rocks while the sea birds swooped and called. Just behind her, Liza too had stopped.

"Isn't it wonderful?" She asked.

"Perfect," replied Liza, in her sweet Irish accent.

The narrow path wound upward to the top of the cliff. Sea and sky appeared to merge and were as if shaded a tinge of sapphire blue, glittering against the beaming sunlight. The air was clear and fresh with the salty smell of the sea. The coast was utterly deserted; indeed, giving the impression that they were completely cut off and alone in the world.

"Come on. Let's go to the top, lazy bones, and then we can stop for a while."

The vivacious expression on Liza's face suddenly changed and gleamed in delight, followed by a reassuring laughter. Emma found herself smiling back at her once again. It was strange, she reflected, how sometimes—though not often, only sometimes —how it was possible to strike an instant rapport with a virtual stranger. She had only met Liza the evening before, and yet, she already felt as if they were very old friends.

She turned and set off up the path again. Nestled at the foot of the cliffs, the little hotel where they were both staying, now resembled a doll's house from this height. Emma had been staying there for almost a week and Liza, for a day or so. It was only the previous evening, over a bottle of mineral water, in the tiny cosy hotel bar, that they had first met and started to talk, and over a short period of time, started to talk and discovered common ground that had drawn them instantly together.

In this day and age, she supposed, it wasn't such an unusual story—but it was somehow reassuring to know that hers wasn't the only life that was, as she thought of it, a typically modern mess—a good job, bad marriage, messy and painful divorce and now, perhaps inevitably, a hopeless affair with a married man.

Liza understood. After all, she had been there *twice!*

"He won't leave—they never do," she had said, playing with her glass, her face sober. Dear, gentle, confused Jamie. He would be here on Friday. He had promised. In spite of herself, Liza's heart lurched at the thought of seeing him.

A couple of days together, here, where no one knew them, where they could walk along the beaches and cliffs, just the two of them, hand in hand, openly, where they could eat out together, laugh together and sleep together, just like a normal couple. And then? Back to reality. Back to Wendy who had devoted her life to him and who must not be hurt. The two children whose education must not be disrupted. And for her, back to an empty flat, an empty life and a telephone that wouldn't ring.

The path was now badly eroded, the stark rock before them, slippery and dangerous.

"Flagging?" Beside her, Liza grinned, impishly.

"Come on—onward and inward, as they say." Perhaps she should end the affair. Perhaps she should say, *'her or me?'* But she couldn't. Because she knew what the answer would be. How many times had he said it?

"Darling, you don't understand. I love you. You *know* I love you. But Wendy is my wife. The mother of my children." Lucky Wendy.

The sun was rising high in the sky, dazzling and hot. She looked up. Liza had clambered up the last steep slope and now stood directly above her on the cliff-top, hands on her hips, silhouetted against the blazing sky.

"Come on. The view is wonderful!"

The footing was treacherous. Part of the path had eroded and slipped away; the edge was perilously close. A bit like life, Emma thought, fleetingly.

Carefully, and a little nervously, she felt her way, suddenly aware of the abyss below her. The path hadn't looked this steep or difficult from below. It had been Liza's idea to come this way. After all, she *had* been here before and knew the path well. Emma noticed, a little belatedly, that Liza's strong walking boots were rather more suited to the terrain than her worn and shabby trainers. She hoped that there was another way down.

The last few yards were steeper than ever, almost a climb. The cliff edge was crumbling, parts of it held together only by turf. However, there was one safe place to climb over to. She reached up forcefully for a handhold.

One of Liza's boots, lightly at first, but with a steady and increasing pressure, stepped on Emma's fingers. She gasped.

"Liza, don't be an *idiot!* This is no time to play stupid games!"

Her voice was cool and soft, almost gentle and soothing, against the distant wash of the sea.

"Oh, and by the way, my name *isn't* Liza; It's Wendy Cartright. Ring any bells?"

Emma's feet were now starting to slip from beneath her. The relentless pressure on her clutching hand was causing it to slip. Frantically, she scrabbled around with her other hand, looking desperately for a safe handhold. Too late. She saw Wendy move and place a rock in her hand. Wendy shook her head, sorrowfully, her eyes dreamy.

"You were really *very very* silly, you know. To write that letter. And to write it on the hotel note-paper."

Wendy leant forward, heavily grinding her foot on Emma's knuckles. She lifted the rock and said,

"Shame; I rather liked you. Still—you know what they say—life's a bitch. And then, you die. Oh, and I'm sure that Jamie would want me to give you his love."

This time, a triumphant, yet lamenting moan, sounded again as Wendy changed into a small country woman with auburn hair and red clothes; namely, a Banshee spirit which Emma could actually see through. And the last words she uttered were, "I am the messenger of your death. Goodbye!"

And as she kicked Emma off the cliff and sent her reeling to her death, she screamed out aloud just before her body crashed far below onto the jagged rocks and was dragged away by the sea like a rag doll.

The End

Death Call: A Samurai Ghost's Recollection of His Death (Japanese Haiku-Poem)

"I was surrounded by Monsters of all shapes and sizes; trapped inside a secret room,

thinking myself safely hidden away and free from danger; but alas they discovered me and so…

I had no option but to raise my Samurai Sword, to avoid being eaten alive, and committed hara-kiri."

Yokai

Japan, Tokyo and inside their parents' exotic and simple, beautifully decorated home, a husband and wife, now both in their mid-fifties were sitting relaxed, comfortably on the floor, both barefooted and in light Spring Clothing. It was mid-day and they were trying to stay cool in the shade during an intense heat-wave, gazing through the sliding open door facing their courtyard at the beautiful and elegant pink leaved tree.

"You know, Yoshimi, I still remember planting that tree with Mum, when I had just turned nine. It seems like only yesterday; how the time flies. Can you recollect what you were doing at the time?"

There was no response. He turned to her and gave her a gentle prod. She seemed lost in thought, staring at the tree and then began to softly sing out, stamping her barefeet on the floor with full force:-

"For the dead won't wake until it starts to get late, oh Yokai! Oh Yokai! For the dead won't wait until it starts to get late, oh Yokai! Oh Yokai! For the dead won't wait until it starts to get late, oh Yokai! Oh Yokai!"

He looked at her, bewildered and then gave her a prod.

"Yoshimi. Why are you acting in such an estranged manner?" asked Yudhishtira.

She suddenly turned towards him and her head morphed into that of a turtle with golden-yellow eyes, then swiftly back to normal, after which, an ecstatic smile formed across her face and she asked very casually.

"Oh Yudhi," she said, waving her beautiful Japanese fan, "I just remembered, I'd prepared some sushi for you in the kitchen. Don't worry, I've prepared it simple especially for you, as you're a vegan so it's small balls of cold rice, garnished with vegetables." "Now you wait right here and I'll serve it to you; sayonara!" She said, giggling, took a bow and waved her hands.

Before he could react, she rose to her feet and left for the kitchen. He rubbed his eyes in disbelief.

"Did I *really* see what I just did!?" "No, it must be my imagination; most likely a hallucination caused by this heat." He shrugged it off then called out,

"While you're there, my love, could you please kindly bring me some beer as well? Thank you, Yosh." He grinned and lay flat on the floor with a pillow.

Before long, she returned, holding a tray with all the food and drink displayed. She smiled and knelt down, carefully placing it on a low table. Yudhi looked at her again, and caressed her hair.

"What is it, Yudi? You're eyes are filling with tears. Is everything alright?"

"I'm sorry, Yoshima. I was just thinking of our parents." He rose to his feet and reached out for a Family Album from a cabinet. He opened it and gazed at their wedding photos. He then sat beside her and they began to look through it.

"It's really amazing and so romantic how Mum and Dad met." He said.

"Yes, when Dad was a single bachelor, in Japan, Tokyo, he was sent on an official tour to India, New Delhi, where he met Mum." Responded Yoshimi.

"Hmm, and that is when they met and it was love at first sight." He looked at her and smiled. "Hey, you never could pronounce my full name, Yudhishtra, but it's alright, I love it how you call me Yudhi." They both smiled and hugged then ate their lunch. Just then, Yoshimi faded into thin air and in a few seconds, re-appeared.

"Everything alright, Yudhi? You look as if you've seen a ghost!" She giggled and poked him.

He jumped and shook in fear.

"Oh, Yudhi, you're trembling."

"I...I think I'll go and take a bath."

Yudhi stood up and made his way to the bathroom. Along the way, he joined his hands in prayer at a statue of Lord Buddha.

"Oh Buddha, please give me the strength to remain positive and only do good Karma."

As he turned around the corner, he looked up on the wall at a mounted Samurai Sword, which had once been owned by one of his great ancestors and fell into his father's hands.

"I always feel uneasy looking at you." He said, to the sword, then retreated to the bathroom.

Once Yudhi was stark naked, he dipped his toes in the tub then entered slowly. The water was warm. He felt so relaxed, that his eyes closed. He smiled.

"Aah, this is pure Heaven. No devils in here. Hah hah."

Suddenly, the bathroom door slid open and a ghostly apparition appeared right in front of him and let out a loud scream.

"Aaaaaaaaaaaaaaaaaaaaaaaaaaaaahhhhhhhhhhhhh!!!!!!!!!!!!!"

Yudhishtra's eyes burst open and he found himself in a tub full of blood and torn limbs. A decapitated head bobbed in the tub along his left arm.

"Euuuhhhh!!!!" In panic, he fell out the tub then noticed the figure blocking the door.

"The devil!!! Aaaaahhhhh!!!"

"I am Shikako, the evil and naughty twin sister of your beloved wife, Yoshimi…and I am going to haunt you to death." She called out in a hollow and eerie voice that echoed across the walls.

"Hah hah hah hah hah!!!"

He closed his eyes tightly and ran through the apparition and into the main room, slipping stark naked on the floor.

"Everything alright, Yudhi. Oh! You're completely naked." She giggled and rushed to get a towel then stopped in her tracks. Her head changed into the same turtle who called out.

"Or maybe you prefer to stay as you are." Then it changed back to her again.

"You…you're shape-shifting and continually possessing animal features…just like a Kappa. Yes…and that monstrosity in the bathroom must be mononoke spirit. It said it was your twin sister called Shikako; but how is that possible. Oh great Buddha, please save my sanity."

"I'm no expert in Japanese mythology, but even a simple girl like me knows they are properly referred to as Yokai!" She rubbed his hair then said,

"Now, I will get you some rice and green tea for your meal, Yosh, and we can talk it over then, hmm?" He opened his mouth to reply, but she had left for the kitchen, giggling. No sooner had she left when blood began to drip from all around the ceiling borders. He stood up alarmed and called out, "Yoshimi!" He rushed to the Kitchen to find it empty and looked around frantically.

"Hey, handsome. Look above you!" He turned his head up and saw Shikako glued to the ceiling in a see-through flesh-coloured robe. Her mouth opened wide and she vomited out a yellow froth that soaked through his stark-naked body.

"Yudi! Ready for your meal, my sweet brother?" It was Yoshimi. Just then, everything turned back to normal and he found himself in a blue robe and seated cross-legged on the floor. She giggled.

"Decided to wear some clothes after all? I quite preferred you without them." She winked and lay out the food on the table at floor level and joined him. He stared at her, wide-eyed and nodded.

"Yoshima: do you think I'm normal?"

"Of course. Why do you say such things? Is something troubling you?"

He looked up at the ceiling and pointed.

"While you were in the Kitchen, I noticed blood all around our ceiling walls and…Shikako was stuck up there."

"Stop!! I don't expect such talks from you. I'm going to forget what I heard and demand that you act normal and eat your meal this instant."

He looked at her and caressed her hair then they ate their meal.

That night, Shikoku appeared once more, lying beside him on the floor. He awoke in a sweat and then vanished into thin air.

"I've made up my mind. There's only one thing left for me to do. I have to go to Dad's secret basement and look for his journals of Exorcism. There will definitely be a clue there. Please forgive me." He tiptoed barefeet and peered across the floor at the other side of the bedroom where his sister Yoshima lay in deep sleep.

"Good. I think I'll go down to the basement now."

Once there, he nodded his head and brushed his hands through his hair.

"Damn. There's a heavy lock across it and it's corroded as well. I'll need to break that chain with something...but what?" He thought for a while and then:-

"Of course! Dad's samurai sword!!!" He tiptoed quietly to the wall and carefully removed it with the greatest of care then returned to the lock. After this, with one swift strike, he struck it against the chain which shattered into tiny pieces. He smiled, then bent down to pull open the door.

A flight of steps ran down, blanketed with total darkness.

"I need a light." "Oh, wait, there's a lantern on a hook, against the first step. Dad always was a great organiser."

As he made his way down with the lantern, which magically lit up itself, he observed that each step he walked on turned to a multitude of different bright colours. First red, then blue, then green, then yellow, then orange, which illuminated the room and made it easier for him to soon reach the massive room where there was a desk. On the desk lay a large heavy red and yellow book.

Yudhi approached the desk and placed the lantern on it then read the book cover.

"My Journal of the Shoku Nihongi history (c. 797) and My Encounters with A Hosishi Exorcist. officiating burial ceremonies for Emperor Konin (781) and Emperor Kanmu (806): by Toshiro Raiki."

"What a long title: typical of Dad!"

He turned the first page which he read out softly:

"I have summoned this estranged exorcist at the burial ceremony of my wife Parineeti." "No! It can't be possible; that's Mum!" "It means…he was trying to bring her back to life! B…but how can this be possible. Even this creepy unnamed exorcist lived so many centuries ago. He can't be a human surely."

He flicked the pages forwards and saw some magic spells.

"Mantra to summon the dead."

Just then, he heard a loud thud. It was the basement door. Somehow it had been shut. He also heard the sound of moving chains and a bolt securing the door. He was trapped inside.

Just then, Shikoko appeared…and beside her stood none other than his own sister, Yoshima, holding a plate of rice.

"Yosh! That's the girl I've been telling you about. Her name is Shikako!"

Yoshima turned to Shikoko. A moment's silence and then, both of them burst into a fit of manic laughter. After which, they closed in on him. Shikako gazed at the book. Her eyes turned to a bright red and flames of fire burst out and burnt the book to cinders. She then turned to their victim.

"You walked right into our trap. You even allowed us to destroy that book. Now, it is time for you to die." She turned to Yoshima.

"I hope you're not a vegan, my sweet sister?"

Yoshika giggled and morphed and slowly began to change into a reptilian animal. She hissed and drool came out her mouth, dripping onto the floor.

"Let's not wait any longer. I'm soooo hungry!" She hissed. "Ssssss!"

"A feast of delicious human-vegan sushi!" Cried out Shikako, hysterically.

Firstly, Shikoko reached forwards, pulled and tore out his entire tongue, after which they spat out venom simultaneously. Finally, tearing him apart very very slowly, fingers first, then toes, then all body parts which they relished and enjoyed.

Before long, all that remained was a heap of bones which they used as ornaments to decorate themselves and display as a lesson…and as a warning *never* to challenge their kind, known as The Yokai.

The End.

Hallowed Cauldron

Deep down below, underneath an Ancient Cornish Cathedral, in a cellar, a small clan, or close-knit group of buried Witches, had been unwittingly revived from vibrations and disturbance from a drill press machine. The first to awaken from the clan of 'dead' sisters was their leader, namely, Hareena the Orange Witch Queen. Her dry shrivelled body stood up wearily from the earth and she stretched her body. Some of the rubble landed over her cloak and her eyes turned a bright orange and she gazed up furiously to where the sounds were, after which she chanted a black magic. She then raised both her arms upwards and, using her sorcery, sent a blaze of white hot flames that sent them burning alive in agony. Still weary after her long sleep, she limped up to a bronze object that had also been unearthed. It was a large metallic cauldron: the same one they had used previously.

Once all the clan were revived, she peered around at them.

"Greetings, my sisters. I trust you are all well. Now that we have risen from our long sleep, it has come to my physic knowledge that the humans are celebrating Halloween. Well, I have decided that we're going to teach them a lesson and make *this particular* Halloween one that they shall never forget and dread ~ *for eternity!*" There was a moment's silence, after which she added,

"We will conjure forth the worst monstrosities from the deepest and darkest pits of Hell. There will be Mummies, Zombies, Ghouls, Vampires, Werewolves, Demon Queens, Hells Clowns, Ogres, Creeps, Witches, Cats and Big Black Bats and many many more!" She cackled wickedly...and, I may add, this time, we won't get our hands bloodied. We will control these monstrosities with our witchcraft and use them to do our work on our Hallowed Cauldron.

The witches stamped their feet and banged their broomsticks in a frenzy, up and down.

"Now, my dark sisters, gather around the black magic cauldron and I will give you all instructions on your tasks."

"Firstly, I want you all to collect the ingredients required to prepare a potion in our cauldron of torture to enable our black magic to work best. That is the reason why I have summoned you all here tonight to appoint this heinous task, as we all need to work together to optimise our power to its fullest potential!"

Hareena then turned to the nearest witch before her.

"Cursella, I need a teenage virgin to boil alive in the cauldron. We can wear the sacrificial bones as ornaments to frighten off onlookers and enjoy the taste of its warm blood."

Cursella bowed her head and knelt before Hareena.

"Oh, and this time, please ensure you *don't* eat the heart as we need it!"

She nodded, then closed her eyes, did a vanishing spell and was gone.

Hareena then turned to a pair of twin sister-witches and smiled with an evil glint in her eyes.

"Totura and Sadista, *for years* you've been waiting for my consent to allow you to roam freely in the night skies; well, now's your chance."

"I'll give you a nice easy one for starters." She ushered them to her and whispered instructions in their ears. Their eyes lit up and they rubbed shoulders gazing into each others eyes, excitedly.

"Aunty Hareena...*you couldn't possible mean*...toasted human flesh coated with essence of brain?"

Sadista frowned and tugged her: "What about the heart?"

Hareena grinned at her nieces, affectionately and said: "Yes yes, brain and heart! And remember to share then bring back some of the 'leftovers' as we need it for our brew." She cackled and her nieces gave her a huge hug.

She then turned to the eldest witch Ghouldra.

"Now, I have something very special for you, Ghouldra." She turned towards her and whispered in her ear, after which she returned to her "as it's fast approaching midnight, you can all take flight; and may the forces of darkness be with you." She cackled out aloud and her voice echoed from corner to corner.

*****

Meanwhile, at their home, a pair of twin sisters, dressed as the brides of Frankenstein and Dracula were making their way out the door to go trick or treating.

"Carra, are there really demons out there? I mean to say...do they *really* exist, or just a made-up thing."

"Of course, Tarra; How many times do I need to remind you. They're just as real as you and I. Now put your coat on quickly and let's go; after all, you don't wanna miss the Mummy and the Zombie double-duo do you?" She laughed wickedly, raising her long black painted nails at her.

"You really do enjoy scaring the pants out of your little sister don't you, Carra!"

Outside, it was cold and there was an abundance of thick fog that blanketed them.

"Oh look. I thought I noticed a bogeyman in the distant horizon!" Said Tarra.

"Huh. Where, where?!" Asked Carra, wide-eyed. Tarra burst into a fit of laughter.

"I hate you. You…you sadist."

Just then, Tarra's laughter faded as she noticed a bandaged figure at the end of the street. It was making its way straight towards them. Carra pointed.

"Next you'll be telling me that *that* Mummy is real and going to kill us. Well, dear sister, you can't fool me this time. Look, I'll prove it!"

*****

Meanwhile, back in the cellar, Hareena's eyes lit up.

"Oh, how could I have overlooked Wizard Oni! I will summon him from the cauldron itself, using my telepathic powers.!"

Suddenly, the cauldron began to fill with smoke from which a tall bearded figure emerged. He wore a long cloak with sparkling stars and had golden eyes with red pupils.

"Greetings Witch-Queen Hareena." He took a bow and looked around, after which he closed his eyes to read her thoughts.

She crossed her fingers and waited in baited breath for his response. After some time, his eyes fluttered open and he raised his eyebrows and said wryly,

"I approve; but do you *really* need me when you and your witch-clan are enough to cause havoc and mayhem?"

"The more the merrier…and besides, only you have enough sorcery to summon forth monstrosities as large as sky-demons."

"True." He said, scratching his chin. "Very well. So, tell me now, what would you like me to do?"

She cackled and whispered something in his ear.

The fog had thickened as Carra who was locked in her sister's grip.

"Don't be foolish, Tarra!"

"Let me go, stupid!" She tugged and pulled to free herself as Carra tried to make a run with her.

"Don't you want to introduce me to your new boyfriend?" She giggled. The Mummy heard this and moved faster towards them, with widened eyes.

In one last desperate bid, with all her might, Tarra slapped her sister on the left cheek and broke free from her then ran off in the opposite direction just as the Mummy reached them.

For a moment, Carra gazed up at the tall bandaged figure. There was a foul stench of decay coming from his.

"Listen, I get the make-up and costume. After all, it is Halloween. It's truly awesome believe me, but I really think you ought to have bathed and brushed your teeth before dating me sister."

Just as the Mummy raised its flaking hand up to strike, an eerie voice called out.

"Not this one. She is not a virgin." The Mummy retreated and walked past her, as if nothing had happened and disappeared into a thick blanket of fog.

The voice had belonged to one of the witches controlling him, namely Cursella.

*****

Elsewhere, at a late-night Fancy Dress Halloween Party Hall, mostly teenagers, people were having wicked fun, playing party pranks and enjoying the Halloween snacks and drinks. It was in full-swing. A girl-ghoul and her Zombie boyfriend were locked in embrace and on a date.

"Lucy, I have something I wanna show you."

"Don't we all!" Quipped Lucy, and burst out in giggles and took a sip of her punch, which her partner Johnny had spiked.

"Oh, you are naughty, but I mean I have something to give you." As he reached out in his left side pocket. Just then, a voice called out from above,

"Look out, here I come!!!"

A witch flew down in her broom stick and landed two slaps on him. The party guests were so engrossed in their fun that nobody seemed to notice.

"That was just for starters, young man. Now, I have something for you!"

Johnny retreated back.

"W…who are you!? Did you actually just fly down from a broomstick?"

"I'm your new date and my name is Ghouldra. Now, you must be punished for staying out so late past your bedtime. A good whipping is what you need."

Witch Ghouldra used her witchcraft to summon a large whip and began whipping Johnny. At first, it was mild and Johnny found it kinky, but then the whipcracks were struck more forcefully. Ghouldra let go and the whip magically worked itself, whipping him constantly. The onlookers clapped, and whistled, enjoying 'the act' and it wasn't long before Johnny's skin began to tear and peel off his body. Ghouldra cackled and produced a bottle of salt and tossed it over his flesh then massaged him vigorously. He yelled and screamed. The party guests clapped louder and stamped their feet begging for more, unaware that this was very real.

Gruella then plucked out his eyes and pulled out his tongue and placed it in her bag and waved to everyone and flew off, leaving Johnny's corpse on the floor. After she left, Lucy approached him cautiously and called out.

"Johnny, you can quit the act and get up now. Come on, I want to go home!" She kicked him and he didn't respond.

"Oh my God. Aaaahhhhhh!!!!"

Meanwhile, elsewhere, Tortura and Sadista had unleashed a zombie to do their 'bloody' work as a pair of lovers made their way past a cliff.

"Oh Andy, how far do we have to go?"

"Not far, according to the map, the ancient castle is plotted out just a few more yards from where we are, Marlene. It shouldn't be hard to sight. Just look out for the stone quarries surrounding it!"

"Maybe we should ask that fellow in the distance. He looks lost!" Said Marlene, pointing to her far right.

Andy and could just make out a figure in the darkness, kneeling on the earth.

"He looks like a scrounger. I think its best we move along."

Marlene stamped her foot in protest, removed her shoes and began making her way towards the figure.

"Ouuchh!!!" She fell on the damp grass in pain and held her right foot, studying the sole.

"Marlene! Are you alright?" Andy rushed to her aid, knelt down and examined her. He noticed a sharp metallic pointed object embedded in her foot sole.

"It looks quite large for a splinter. Hold tight, I'm going to try and pry it out."

Marlene closed her eyes tightly and gripped Andy's shoulders.

"Aaarrhhh!" She screamed and then, after a few moments, was calm.

Andy examined the object more closely. It depicted two people being attacked and decapitated by someone or something sinister. He turned pale.

"What is it, Andy? You look like you'd seen a ghost."
"Show it to me."

"N-no. It's just some sick inbred playing a sick prank on us."

Marlene then spotted something very unusual. The figure was now tearing out clumps of earth and seemed to be feasting on it.

"Are you going to help that poor fellow or should I?"

Andy stood up, annoyed. "Alright, it seems I have no choice. Tell you what, you make your way to the castle and I'll bring our friend along shortly, satisfied?"

Marlene smiled and kissed him, then headed forwards. Once she was out of his view, Andy made his way to the figure and noticed that his head was in the earth. He dug his hands in his pocket and pulled out a partially eaten sandwich. He reached out and tapped his back to draw his attention, but when he turned and looked up suddenly. Andy jumped, then stood his stance and smirked.

"Oh! Now I get it. This must be your idea of a Halloween prank. Gosh, I should have brought my silver cross with…" Just then, the figure grabbed both his legs and pulled him down forcefully then began tearing him apart vigorously.

"No. Nooo. Aaaahhh!!"

Just above them, Tortura and Sadista were enjoying the bloody sight and decided to intervene. Tortura cast a spell that sent the zombie sinking down into the earth, burying it. She then removed the brain and the heart, placed it in her cloak and smirked at Sadista.

"Finally, Aunty Hareena gave us an opportunity to enjoy ourselves. Come on, we had better head back as it's fast approaching dawn." They took flight on their brooms.

Later that night, in the cellar, all the witches had gathered with their collections and placed them inside the Hallowed Cauldron where Queen Hareena stood with a wry grin across her face. Each of the witches took a bow after doing so.

"Ah, my nieces are back! And how was your first flight out?"

In response, Tortura and Sadista smiled wickedly and handed her the bag containing the blood-soaked brain and the heart.

"Of course, that was just a warm up exercise." She cackled wickedly, tossing them in the Hallowed Cauldron.

"Our potion is now ready" then she turned to Wizard Oni who had just joined her and raised her arms high up in the air and screamed out.

"Let the Nightmare begin! Unleash the monstrosities!!!"

The End?

The Bleached Eyes of a Torn Soul

I do not struggle to feel
My feelings flow through my veins
I see a dark, cold and barren place: desolate
Mists of lilaq that smell hauntingly pleasant
My senses have foreseen predictions of reality
A place for lost souls is my fate
My soul has cried again and again to a point of insanity
The bleached eyes of a torn soul never to be realised
Death is my companion and I am ahead in TIME
Death has placed her icy fingers along my body several times
A poem of fears is my destiny
I see endless gravestones and among them is my own
Here lies the body of a miserable and crumbled soul
I forsee visions of a spiritual nature
I am safe here in an unknown dimension
I am a ghost, but an unhappy one
Where I am going to is a place of peace
There shall be others like me, crying and thinking
It's so cold, dark and lonely; but there is a sense of freedom
I belonged somewhere, once upon a time
There is no daylight, just darkness
Occasionally, looming ghosts of dead people stroll free of will

No communication, only tears and pain of leaving loved ones behind.
Why I'm here and where my next fate lies, remains a mystery…

Witches' Blood

"Oh betrayer of my true-love
Judas re-incarnated
How does it feel
Living with a guilty conscious
for the remaining part of your life?"
"GOD is watching you
As you make bad-karma"
"Oh betrayer of my true-love
Your fate is now sealed
And you'll surely get what you deserve
As a consequence of your evil deeds."
"Oh betrayer of my true-love
My so called 'soul-mate'
How does it feel
Living in fear
Of being exposed for who you really are"
"Oh betrayer of my true love
You have played with my innocency and feelings
Surely you are among the lowest of the lowest.
May your wicked plan fail and
May you *never* find peace, love and happiness
For what you did to me,
For I am your Victim and this gave you

Sadistic power and happiness."
"I pour Holy Water over your evil memories
To wash away your Witches' Blood,
AMEN."

Wail of the Scarecrow

This Halloween Night, stay well clear of the open field and make your way back safely to your homes quickly making sure you lock and bolt all windows and doors because tonight is All Soul's Eve and the Gates of Hell are wide-open and the Scarecrows are going "walkies"
They're hungry for human flesh and thirsty for blood
Run for your life I plead with you, when you hear…
The Wail of the Scarecrow!
Befriending Loneliness:
(What the Lonely Clown told me that Halloween Night)
Loneliness is my only friend and
She will never leave me.
Always by my side;
In darkness, as well as in the light,
Yes, loneliness is my real friend.
Befriending Loneliness
I'm Befriending Loneliness
Time after time, again and again,
Love has betrayed me,
Leaving me hurt and rejected,
But you were always there for me.
Yes, Loneliness is my one and only true friend to the very end.

Duppy

Yet another bloody, mutilated and gruesome murder victim had been discovered by LIT, whose abbreviations stood for the Law Investigation Team. It was headed by Detective Fuji Yamaha, a robust man in his mid-thirties with a paralysed left leg. The scene of the murder posed a riddle.

Gory and disturbing and difficult to interrogate, bloodied and mutilated body parts were deliberately planted neatly across the network of paths and hedges which made up the sections of a massive 'Maze of Phantom Spectres', located in a Funhouse Theme Park.

Just then, Detective Fuji's mobile phone sounded its familiar bell tone. It was a text message that read:

"The fun has only just started. Enjoy the show! ~ Duppy."

'The Maze Serial Killer' had just announced his arrival…

Detective Fuji turned to one of his team members, a young lady in her twenties.

"Ms Stobo, I want this place closed to the public immediately."

The body was soon identified as that of a teenage girl aged eighteen, named Sarah Pastel, the elder daughter of Henry Pastel, a retired Art Lecturer who now ran his own business; a shop named Pastel's Portraits. Now in his late sixties, he was hoping to hand over his business to Sarah, a budding artist herself; until her murder. Henry was left in complete shock and disbelief.

"No, I can't accept Sarah could just leave me this way. Impossible. I need to go out and look for her." He suffered from various health-problems, which included arthritis, so his walk was slow and painful. Nonetheless, life moved on and he had to make a living. He reached the door to revert the 'Open' sign to 'Close' and was about to open the door to leave when then felt a warm hug around his waist. It was Bertha, his younger daughter, who was just thirteen.

"Oh, Daddy. Henry turned to see her. Her eyes appeared so calm and angelic.

He stroked her medium-length auburn hair softly. Then his expression changed and he said aloud, "Bertha, don't stop me now. I have to go and look for your sister. Aren't you the slightest bit concerned for her welfare?"

"Daddy, you know I am. She was my sister."

"Listen to me, Bertha. Those 'remains' were not Sarah's."

Just then, the door opened and Detective Fuji entered. He removed his hat and bowed his head.

"I'm sorry, Mr Henry, but the decapitated blood-soaked head was that of your daughter, Sarah. I'm afraid I'm going to have to order you to remain here for your own safety. This is a private case involving a serial killer. I've taken the liberty of placing police guards around your shop. I assumeyou and your daughter live here." He turned to Bertha.

"And it was you, wasn't Bertha, who identified her. She nodded.

Just then, Detective Fuji's eyes fell to the floorboards and he noticed something.

"I can see one of your customers had extra-large feet." They all stared at them.

"Dad! ~ Called out Bertha. "I never noticed anyone come in since morning."

Detective Fuji grimaced and scratched his chin thoughtfully.

"Do you have a log-book, where you record all the customers who come in."

"Of course! Cried Bertha. CCTV. We can check it. It's in my room." He smiled.

"Listen, I admire a bluestocking intelligent young lady. Thank you, but I must emphasise that this is a private investigation so I need to work only with my team on this case, strictly on duty." "Now, you don't mind if I contact my colleague."

"No, of course not. Please go ahead." Said Henry. He placed both his hands into his daughter's reassuringly and said softly.

"It's alright, darling. Let them do their work. We just need to cooperate."

Detective Fuji spoke on his mobile.

"Ms Stobo, it's alright, you can come in now. I need you to help me operate the CCTV."

"I'm in the back of the shop you idiot!!!" Replied a hoarse voice. Then the phone disconnected.

"How strange. She never spoke to me like that before."

There was a moment's silence and then, Detective Fuji's eyes filled with fear and he turned tothem.

"Where's the back exit."

"This way." Replied Beha and led the way.

Outside, he looked around frantically and saw a smashed up mobile phone.

"Ms Stobo!!

"Where are you?"

"Aaaahhhhh!!!" Screamed Bertha. Detective Fuji turned and headed towards her. She was staring at a pool of blood where a skinned and start lady sat crouched, covering her face.

"Ms Stobo…is… that you?"

She looked up at him instinctively to reveal a skinned and mauled face with eyeballs popped out, after which, the skinned semi-living corpse began to sing:

"La la la la laa, He's out to get you And is on the prowl tonight, Terrifying all that come in his path Better to lock your windows and doors tonight Coz' Duppy's coming to get you. La la la laa laa."

After which, her body slumped sideways, lifeless into a heap, like a contorted doll.

Bertha looked away, sickened while Inspector Fuji removed his hat, bowed his head then took off his coat and covered the body.

He then contacted Headquarters.

"Hello, this is Detective Fuji. This is an Emergency. I want a couple of police officers here right away. It's a Pastel's Portraits, a corner shop, first turn from the Funhouse Theme Park.

There's also a body here. I want a post-mortem autopsy performed immediately."

He then turned to Bertha and looked at her, seriously~

"Bertha, it's not safe for you and your father to remain here alone. You need Police protection."

"Mr Pastel, I want you to close the shop during the investigation."

"This is ridiculous. So it means my daughter and I are prisoners in our own shop."

"I don't want any arguments. The point is…you are ALIVE."

Detective Fuji then pointed his mobile on a set of the footprints and snapped a photograph then walked to the door, flipped the Open sign over so it read Closed, smiled reassuringly and said,

"I'll be in touch. Stay safe."

"Oh father, what about my studies. I have to attend college. I can't just…"

"Let's go in the kitchen and fix up a warm meal then think about what we can do afterwards."

Before long, police guards were standing outside. Henry and Bertha decided to get some sleep.

*****

The following morning, at the Police Station, a bony middle-aged lady entered barefoot and looked around. Her body was covered with tattoos and she wore a dark blue cloak with red skulls over them.

A police lady approached her.

"Yes, what can I do for you?"

"I must speak with Detective Fuji."

"What's it regarding?" She inspected her from head to toe.

"The murders. You could say, I'm a witness."

Just then, Detective Fuji appeared. He was relishing a vegan burger with some French Fries.

"Please come into my office er..."

"I'm a high priestess, but you may call me Madam Xoozi Hara, pronounced with a Z"

"Follow me please."

Once inside, he asked her to be seated but she declined and sat cross-legged and closed her eyes.

"Please, Madam Xoozi Hara, make yourself comfortable."

She smiled then inhaled deeply and began to rise mid-way in the air then stopped and opened her eyes. Detective Fuji dropped his lunch on the floor and stood gaping in disbelieve.

"Oh, I know. You must be one of those magicians. Hah, you ought to be on a talent show.

Anyway, please tell me what you know about the murders."

"He cannot die. He is already dead.

"What?!"

"Duppy: He is not a mortal. He's an apparition. You can never stop him...ever." For a moment,

her eyeballs turned gold, then back to hazel brown again.

"Enough of your tricks, Madam Xoozi. You're wasting valuable police time. There's a sick twisted maniac, a serial killer out there and you're performing magical feats in my office. Please leave."

Her eyes filled with rage.

"Foolish man. You think I am bluffing. I will prove to you that I am real. Now, focus your mind on your left leg which is paralysed."

She stared at it and began to chant some mantra in an unusual language. Then reached out both her arms. Suddenly, electric sparks fired at it then stopped.

"Now; can you feel the sensation in it?"

Detective Fuji placed his hands over it and pressed. His face lit up and he smiled in ecstasy.

"You...you cured it." He stood up and began to move around on the floor like a young man.

"Thank you so much. Please forgive me."

She smirked and made her way to the door.

"Madam Xoozi. You said you witnessed something. Can you help me in my investigation? We have to stop this serial killer; Dubby."

"Do not mock the dark ones! He is known as Duppy; an apparition. He is a spirit and can appear and disappear as he pleases."

"You seem to know a lot about him. How come?"

"That's because, it's my misfortune that he is my child!!!" She snapped her fingers and vanished.

"What!?"

Suddenly, the door burst open and a police officer entered, trying to catch his breath and spoke, "Lieutenant, there's been another Maze Murder and...all the police guards have been killed."

"What about the girl and her father?"

"They're safe."

"Alright, let's go."

It was late evening by the time they arrived at the 'Maze of Phantom Spectres', Detective Fuji was horrified at the sight before him.

Not only were there butchered body parts, but foul words were curved out on them with a knife.

He felt sick and vomited. Then his eyes lit up.

"Of course. I need to talk to whoever's running this place; the owner." The only problem was that the Funhouse Theme

Park was so massive and he did not have a map. The place was closed to Public, so there was no one he could ask. He clenched his left fist in frustration.

"Damn it. Who owns this place!?"

Suddenly, there was a crackling sound, like an electric current and Madam Xoozi appeared out of thin air and sat cross-legged, floating in the air.

"If you must know, then this place belongs to my son…Duppy!!! And now that you do know, you must prepare to die."

"Oh Duppy dear! Your din-din's ready. Come and eat, before it gets cold!"

Before Detective Fuji could respond, the ground under his feet began to tremble and two decayed arms ripped through the earth and the pale bony hands gripped his legs with a grip of steel and pulled his straight down into the ground.

Silence followed. Unlike the previous murders, this one was clean and silent and no one would ever know and Duppy was now free to come out and kill again or perhaps wait until next Halloween.

What fun that would be!!

The End??